I0688501

PRESIDENTIAL
AFFAIR

THE SENATOR'S SECRET

JENNIFER REBECCA

The Senator's Secret

Copyright © 2019 Jennifer Rebecca

This book is a work of fiction. Names, characters, places, and incidents are the product of the authors' imaginations and are used fictitiously. Any resemblance of actual events, locales, or persons, living or dead, is coincidental.

All rights reserved. Except as permitted under the U.S. Copyright Act of 1976, no part of this publication may be reproduced, distributed, or transmitted in any form or by any means, including photocopying, recording, or other electronic or mechanical methods, without the prior written permission of the author.

Cover Design by
;
Alyssa Garcia
www.upliftingauthorservices.com

Editing by
Kayla Robichaux

For more information about Jennifer Rebecca & her books, visit:
www.jenniferrebeccaauthor.com

THE SENATOR'S SECRET

My carefully crafted life is being threatened.

Someone wants to tarnish my squeaky-clean image. I make my living cleaning up the messes left behind by New York's elite. But what happens when my life becomes the mess I avoid so carefully?

Can I trust the one man I swore to hate forever, the sexy U.S. Senator—*whose name is on everyone's lips and whose body is rumored to be in every woman's bed*—to help me?

I guess a little blackmail never looked so sexy...

For Alyssa,

You're the Shirley to my Laverne,
The Ethel to my Lucy,
The Nutella to my peanut butter,
The Coke to my whiskey,
The best to my friend,
The sister of my heart.

You ground me when I'm adrift.
You keep me going when things get tough.
I love the way you life,
And I am forever grateful to be a part of your family.

#JenandAlyssatravel

CAMELOT HAS ITS QUEEN

PROLOGUE

Crashing Down

"No. No, no, no, no, no!"

This can't be happening. My hands shake as I flip through picture after picture. How could this have happened?

I've been so careful. I have meticulously watched every move I have ever made throughout my entire life. I never drink too much or eat too much. I have never partaken in recreational pharmaceuticals or otherwise. I don't stay out late and party. And every lover I have ever had has been not only respectable but also discreet. *Hell, the last two signed Non-Disclosure Agreements.*

I just don't know how this could've even happened.

My heart is beating so fast in my chest I feel like I might be sick. Drops of sweat are trickling down from my temples and between my breasts, and my skin is flushed hot.

But anyone looking in the windows of my palatial corner office would see exactly what I want them to. This is what I show the world every day, that I am calm, cool, and collected. I keep myself poised and in control no matter what. My hair is pulled back in a perfect ballet bun on top of my head, my makeup is light and tasteful, and my suit is Chanel. I don't play around. I have worked way too hard for my career. My reputation precedes me all over town—and *this* town is an important one.

I let the stack of glossy drug store one-hour prints fall on top of the plain manila envelope they came in where it sits on top of my mahogany desk. In secret, I call it my fancy desk. It sits proud with its elegant scrollwork carved along the edges.

I didn't grow up like this. My parents are respected attorneys here in New York, but I made the family name a commodity in high-power circles, where they need me and desperately want to know me.

I recoil from the envelope as if it's a rattlesnake sitting on my desk and not the stack of worthless paper that it is. But my conscience whispers that it's not worthless. This envelope of pictures could be *very* valuable in the right—or should I say wrong—hands. There are plenty of people here in New York who would just love to get their hands on this caliber of ammunition to use against me.

This package was sent to my office by courier with

my name type-printed on the front and a note inside written in thick block letters.

I'LL BE IN TOUCH.
DON'T SAY A WORD.

I'm sure if I took it to the police, there would be no fingerprints either. But I can't do that. If I go to the police, this will be all over town and it will ruin my reputation. And my reputation is *everything*.

The worst part: I didn't even do it.

I tap the red-painted sole of my black patent leather Louboutins on the carpet. It's the only outward sign of my distress, and I keep that shit thoroughly hidden behind my desk. Now the question is, how do I proceed? I need to figure out what to do to keep my world from crashing down and fast.

I pick up my cellphone—the latest model that hasn't even been announced yet—and slide my carefully manicured index finger up the dark glass. It scans my face and unlocks. I scroll through my contacts until I see the one I don't want to dial with every fiber of my being. I stare it down like it's a bomb ticking down every second before it explodes in my face—just like I know this decision will later—before I finally force myself to take a deep breath and hit the Call button.

"Hello?" a whiskey-smooth voice answers. I hate that the sound of him makes me furious and my panties wet. This is definitely an unwelcome predicament.

"I need your help," I say. The words taste like sawdust on my tongue, and acid churns in my belly.

"What an interesting turn of events," he replies, and I detest how damn happy he sounds. As if my fall from greatness is something to be celebrated. Of course, he doesn't know that my life is hanging precariously in the balance.

"Don't sound so smug," I warn my adversary. "This affects you as much as it does me."

"Like I said—*interesting*. Meet me at the Magic Boarding House Tavern at eight o'clock," he says. "I'll be waiting."

I open my mouth to issue a witty putdown, but I'm too late. A dial sound goes off in my ear, letting me know that slimeball hung up on me.

My only hope now is that he can get me out of this mess. I know it's going to cost me; I just hope it's a price I'm able to pay for in one way or another. And also that I can stay strong and resist a certain U.S. senator with less than questionable morals and his stupid dimples, because sex and blackmail certainly don't mix.

JAKE'S BIG SNAKE TELL-ALL

ONE

Don't look

Thirty-six hours earlier

I knew he would be here.

I turn quickly so Senator Chancellor can't catch my eye. I know it sounds childish, but I just can't stand the man. Actually, it's more than I just can't stand him. He's never been rude or crass to me, quite the opposite actually. He is always charming and polite. He's beyond good-looking, with a he-knows-it arrogance that speaks volumes of his confidence. He's aware of how sexy he is, and so does every woman in a fifty-mile radius.

Maybe that's what bothers me. My grandmother used to tell me that "no one would buy the ice-cream truck if you were handing out popsicles for free out the back." And everyone woman in the tri-state area has had her fill of Jake Chancellor's popsicle—that is, except for me.

I remember when Jake first came back to New York. He'd been stationed all over the world as a Navy SEAL until he suddenly popped up in New York society. His tuxedo, as always, was crisp and custom fit, the scruff that darkened his jaw gave him a forbidding look, and a darkness behind his blue eyes would tell anyone with half a brain to run for the hills. So obviously, that's exactly what I did.

I was just beginning to build my reputation at the firm and had been asked to attend one of these events. I felt the hairs on the back of my neck tingle, and when I turned around, there he was across the room, and he was looking at me. It had felt like he was *only* looking at me. He exuded a dark, stand-back aura. One look at him and you could tell he was dangerous. I like to pride myself on my self-preservation instincts, so I stayed away.

Sometime over the last few years, his rough edges have softened, but I can tell it's all an illusion to make him more palatable for mass consumption. And from what I've heard lately, every woman out there wants to be consumed by him. Truth be told, I would too, but I don't have an adventurous bone in my body. So that leaves me only on the fringes, on the outside looking in.

And once again, I find myself across the room from him, wearing my best pale-pink silk dress and beaded Louboutins. My blonde hair is delicately curled, and my makeup is tasteful but darker than my daytime look thanks to my favorite stylist and friend, Cara. She's new-ish to the city and keeps everything pretty close to the vest, but I like her. I get the sense she's running from something, and God forbid if it's a man, because I have decided she's part of my circle, my tribe, and that means I will make him pay for his crimes with every fiber of my being. That is, if it even is a man.

Don't look… don't look… don't look!

Senator Chancellor winks at me from across the room, and I let out a sigh of frustration as I turn away quickly. Of course Cara's problems stem from a man. *They always do.*

I turn to the mayor of the city, Gordon Samuels.. I need him. Without his help, the Open Arms Project won't even get off the ground. Whether it's building permits or the right connections, I need the Mayor of New York on my side.

"Good evening, Grace," he says as he notices me. "We were just talking about you."

"All good things, I hope." I smile as sweetly as possible.

"Of course," the mayor agrees. "We were just discussing your new pet project."

"Open Arms is sort of a passion project for me," I agree.

"We love that you want to help homeless veterans in the city," Mayor Samuels begins. "I, myself, am a Desert Storm veteran."

"Thank you for your service, sir."

He just winks at me. I really like Mayor Samuels.

"We were just thinking what a great opportunity it would be for you to partner with Senator Chancellor," he says, letting the name of my arch nemesis hangs in the air for the extended amount of time it takes for me to recover.

"I would hate to impose on the senator," I reply, swallowing back the bile that fills my throat. "He is a very busy man."

"That he is," the mayor agrees. "But veterans' organizations are a key point of his platform. I'm sure he'd make an exception for you."

"You mean he'd make an exception for Open Arms," I correct him.

"Yes. That's exactly what I meant."

"Well…" I try to evade the subject politely. I just don't want to work with Jake Chancellor. Is that so much to ask? "Our team seems to have a pretty great handle on things so far. But if we need him farther on down the road, I'll consider it."

The men all seem to exchange pointed looks with each other that I do not like, and worry turns my stomach to acid. I feel a nervous tingle shiver up my spine and look over my shoulder. Senator Chancellor is standing at the bar, and he's watching… *me*.

The bartender passes him a highball glass filled with amber liquid. I heard he's a whiskey drinker, only in moderation, but that he enjoys a glass of the smoky liquor from time to time. I'm mesmerized as his strong hand slowly lifts the glass to his full, sensual lips and he takes a long swallow, showing no signs of the burn. I watch his corded neck as he turns his eyes to me again and blink slowly once… twice….

But my body jerks back as if I've been struck when a gorgeous blonde—not just any blonde, but well-known socialite Ashley Jefferies—sidles up to him and places her hand on his arm, where it rests on the bar top. They know each other in more ways than just joining the same gym or shopping at the same Target. The way she touches him is… intimate. The way that they circle each other hints at the way that they've seen each other naked. And I hate it. I know that I shouldn't. I have absolutely no claim on him—hell, I can't even stand him, but that doesn't mean that I'm not drawn to him.

It's subtle, but by the look on his face, he sees my reaction. I don't want to see a look of pity cross his handsome face and I know that it will, so, I look back to the mayor and his companions.

How could I have been so stupid? How could I have let myself be pulled into his sexual prowess again when I know this… this… alley cat in search for the next available female in heat is exactly who he is? When will I learn? Unfortunately for me, I'll learn that lesson the hard way, with my panties on his bedroom floor and my reputation down the toilet. That is, if I'm not careful. And I will be careful.

I know that to him, I will never be anything but a number, and still, I let him. At least my saving grace is that I've never been pulled as far as his bed. The Senator and I may have circled this dance floor for years now, but I have still never given in.

"W-what were we talking about?" I stammer out my question.

They exchange looks again before answering me. "We just don't feel that we can sign on to support your project, in one way or another, without the senator on board as well," the mayor says, speaking for the group.

"What?" I squeak on barely more than a whisper.

"At this time," the mayor's friend repeats what he just told me, effectively ruining my life, "we just can't move forward without Senator Chancellor. Get him and you have us."

"O-okay," I say woodenly before excusing myself.

I try to rally the rest of the evening, but it's no use. Nearly everyone gave me the same response. Without Chancellor, no money, no support, essentially killing my project. Shell-shocked, I stagger across the ballroom toward the exit. For whatever reason, I look back toward the bar. The senator is there, still watching me, but this time he winks. It's the only indication he knows exactly how my evening has gone, and he is loving every minute of it. For years, I have carefully avoided any connections with Jake Chancellor, and he has made careful maneuvers to place himself in my realm as often as possible. He loves the cat-and-mouse game, and I just want off the ride.

Just then, perfectly polished Ashley of the sexy socialites slides up closer to him and wraps her arms around him in that way that clearly suggests she's ready to find a location with a firm mattress and less clothes involved. I wouldn't be surprised if they don't even make it back to someone's residence. Those two are most likely to make it to a backseat—*if they're lucky.*

She's been after him to put a ring on it for weeks. She's even gone so far as to tell everyone who would listen that she thinks she's going to be the one to lock down Jake Chancellor, a man who has been seen with more women than I even knew resided within a tri-state area. And good for her. I hope she manages to snag him. They probably deserve each other. Evil villains always do. But for me? I'm done. I shake my head and turn away from them, leaving behind the ballroom and all the people in it. Maybe things will go better tomorrow.

Then again, maybe they won't.

WHO COULD
BE THE NEXT
WOMAN TO
GRACE THE
SENATOR'S BED?

TWO

Cats don't talk back

The early morning sun is shining brightly through the sheer curtains that hang in my bedroom window. I lazily stretch my arms over my head and let a satisfied smile spread across my face before my eyes even open. Last night went so well. I just know we're going to make our goal for this project. I just need to push a little harder. I was disappointed last night, but today, I am reinvigorated. I will take on the world.

I almost have the funding and support I need to help Open Arms, a local organization that wants to build an all-service residence for homeless veterans. A place where they can find a safe place to land, find work, and basic medical and mental health resources. It will be a lot like Father Joe's Villages in San Diego, which help homeless teens finish their education and find work.

I first found Open Arms through Purple Paws, which is an animal rescue that partners with the local animal shelters I volunteer at. Purple Paws rescues dogs from high kill shelters and then trains them to be service dogs for wounded veterans. Both organizations are beyond worthy of the support and money New York's elite society can provide them. Not to mention the notoriety. And last night, when I was rubbing elbows with the upper crust, they were all too happy to join my cause.

There was just one problem.

Nearly everyone I talked to suggested I reach out to Senator Chancellor to champion my cause, seeing as how he is the glamourous former Navy SEAL who looks as good in a suit and tie supporting the people of New York as he does in his dress white uniform on the lawn of the White House. And I'm not gonna lie—I have seen him in his dress whites for a special occasion, and panties all across the tri-state area and beyond instantly burst into flames, only to be put out by the flood of moisture from all of the pussies they contained. It was… *intense*. And I am sad to say even I was not completely immune to his big muscles and stupid dimples. I fan my face a little and vow again that I will not fall prey to the sexy senator's magic penis powers.

I won't let it happen again. I am strong. I am an independent woman. I will not bend. I will not fall victim to a sexy man with the love of a nation behind him, because that is a recipe for disaster if ever I saw one. Loving a man who has women lining up around the block cannot be good for one's emotional health and well being.

This makes last night's turn of events a... *slight* setback.

The last few key people I need to secure the funding for Open Arms only want to work with Senator Chancellor. They feel that he will make a great public face for the organization. Even more so, since it falls perfectly in line with several of his campaign promises, where our nation's veterans are concerned. And it's true, he would be great. If I could handle being around his flirty smile and those damn dimples.

No matter how many charming smiles or politely worded pleas I sent their way, it wouldn't get them to budge. I need the king of the alley cats as my partner or no money from the fancy rich people. And we need the fancy, rich people money or else we won't be able to open the veterans' center. I will find a way to get it done without the state's resident manwhore. I swear it. Even if it's the last thing I do before I die. And I may die. Or my vagina will implode. Same thing.

Part of me wonders if that's really fair. Is it my own selfishness that's keeping me from asking the senator for his backing? Or is it self-preservation? I just know that if given half the chance, he would discard me like yesterday's underwear—just like every other woman in the city—and it would gut me. I would be humiliated to be cast aside so casually. And so publicly. And it *would be* publicly, because Jake is a U.S. Senator. He's not only a U.S. Senator; he is the rockstar of all politicians. Jacob Chancellor is fairly young for a politician at forty-three years old. He comes from an old— as in arrived on *the Mayflower* old—New York family. And he's gorgeous. With a body still full of muscles and what's rumored to be fantastic… other parts, he is one of the most sought after celebrities in the city. And let us not forget the fact that the man is a goddamn war hero with more pretty ribbons and shiny medals that he proudly trots out whenever it appeals to him. And why shouldn't he? He earned them as a freaking Navy SEAL. One would never know by looking at his superior physical form, but he has a scar from a bullet wound on his shoulder and some shrapnel in a hip that occasionally causes a limp when it rains—or so I've read in an article in the Post. He is followed everywhere, his every move scrutinized, and I know myself well enough to understand that I cannot handle failure on that public of a stage.

Even if being near him makes my heart beat faster… he makes me angrier than anyone ever has before. The man truly makes my blood boil. He is a boil on the butt of America. A beautiful boil that I need to lance before I fuck it.

"Merow," my cat Spot calls out from beside me.

I turn to look at him. He's standing right next to my head, looking at me. It would be creepy to realize there is a cat standing on the side of my bed just staring at me—that is, if I didn't already have an orange tabby named Subby sleeping on my pillow above my head and gently petting my hair. Somehow, I ended up with the Norman Bates collection of cats, and I don't even know how, they all just kind of found me, one at a time. But I love every single one of these little weirdos. I let out a frustrated sigh and throw the covers back before climbing from my warm and comfy bed.

"All right, all right," I say.

It's clearly feeding time at the zoo—or at least that's what my dad calls my apartment. I make my way down the short hall to the small eat-in kitchen. I pull a stack of eight small bowls down from an upper cabinet, where I put them last night after I washed them, and set it on the counter with the spoon I pulled from the drawer. My heart pangs a little when I see the ninth bowl that is tucked in the back of the cupboard. It's been three months and still I miss Pepper, a solid black cat who had been no less than seventeen pounds. But she was old and she was in pain. It was her time. Jamie, my favorite vet tech, sat with me the entire time, and together we said goodbye to my first fur baby.

Pepper and I had been together since I was a young teen, when I brought home a tiny runt who had been abandoned by her mother and begged my mom to let me keep her. I even told my dad that she was "just visiting," and when he asked how long Pepper would be with us, I had answered him truthfully, that she would be with us forever. Dad laughed at my explanation that "We're all just visiting this world" and proclaimed me a future lawyer, just like him and my mom.

And if love could have saved Pepper, she would have lived forever.

I grab two big cans of cat food from the pantry and set them next to the bowls. As I begin lining up all of the bowls in front of me, the rest of the circus shows up. You would think the way my little kitty tabernacle choir is singing that they are starving, but they are not. They have a huge feeder of dry food and a freaking water fountain to drink out of whenever they please.

I crack open the first can and divide it into quarters to be evenly distributed amongst the first four bowls, and then I do the same with the second can. My kitty army, all lined up in a row like good little soldiers, waits for me to place their bowls in front of all them before they dive in at once. I wouldn't believe it myself if I didn't see it every day. And then I get out of the way.

I open another upper cabinet and pull down my favorite coffee mug. It's white with gold letters that reads **I love Caturday**. Even though it's Sunday, I use it anyway, because it's my absolute favorite with its little kitty face wearing a flower crown painted underneath the letters. I plop it under the spout of my Keurig and hit the blue button that makes my magic brew flow. While the magic happens, I pull open the door to my fridge and search for the bottle of creamer.

My work life may be neat and orderly, but my home life could easily be called chaotic. I like to think it's how I balance the halves of me.

When I finally locate the bottle I was looking for in

between the old takeout containers and instant break-fast egg cups, I pluck it from its hiding spot and pour it into my waiting mug. I toss the bottle back into the fridge and look over my shoulder when a hear another "Meow." All of the cats but one have scattered, leaving just my judgy shadow behind.

"I can figure it out," I tell him. "I don't need the sexy senator to help me get this project off the ground." Spot just sits there, silently disagreeing with me.

I pick up my cup and make my way to the corner of my small living room where my desk sits. I just know that all of my efforts last night will pay off. I am almost completely sure I convinced those power players who were still on the fence to give me their support—with or without the damn dimples and the jerk who owns them. I sit down in my chair and reach for the slim white mouse. I shake it a bit to wake up my computer and log in to my email. And find disappointment.

I let out a heavy sigh and lean back in my chair. I sip my now cool coffee while letting my eyes track over the words I don't want to read. I have to convince them that we do not need Jacob Chancellor. And we don't, right? But there's a part of me that whispers I'm not being fair. That my refusing to work with him is nothing but selfishness and my own irresponsibility.

I can't solve the world's problems like this, so I push back from my desk and make my way down the hall to my bedroom. I brush my teeth while I avoid looking at myself in the mirror, another clear indicator I'm not doing the right thing, and I hate that. I don't want to be this person, and I'm not going to be that person who blames someone else for their lack of moral character. This is clearly my own character flaw.

I brush my hair out and twist it up into a messy bun. I toss my pajamas onto my bed as I make my way to my closet and pull on my favorite pair of well-worn jeans and a long-sleeved T-shirt. I pull my favorite NYU crew neck sweatshirt over my head. It's navy-blue with big light-blue block letters stitched to the front. I slide my feet into a pair of red canvas Toms and head for the door.

I grab my black Michael Kors tote and am rooting around in its deep depths for my keys when I hear my cell phone ring. I race back to the kitchen, pick it up off the counter, and slide my finger across the cool glass screen.

"Hello?"

"Just checking that we're on for dinner tonight," Jules, my college roommate, says when I answer.

"Of course," I reply. We always meet for dinner every other Saturday.

"Excellent!" she cheers. "I want to go to Clear."

I let out a groan. "I was hoping we could go to The High Dive and maybe grab a burger," I admit. While I do love the finer things in life, after all the prep of hairspray, tape, and wallpaper spackle that charity galas like last night's event require, I don't exactly feel like putting in the effort to meet the dress code of one of New York's most elite fine dining restaurants. Unfortunately, Jules loves everything about it. And why wouldn't she? She was bred for this kind of life. I am pretty sure she came out of the womb wearing pearls and heels.

"What?" she gasps. "You love Clear." And I do. I just want something a little different.

"I do," I say hesitantly. I love Jules, and she loves to get dressed up. She would only show up to my favorite hole in the wall place in Dior anyway. "The usual time?"

"Yes! See you there!" She hangs up before I can say anything else, and a quick look at the clock on the microwave tells me I need to hustle to get to the animal shelter if I'm going to make it back home in time to change for our dinner reservation Jules is undoubtedly on the phone making right now.

I toss my phone in my bag and hear the telltale clank of it hitting my keys. I say a silent thanks to the lost keys fairy for helping me when I'm running behind and pull them out. I race out the door and lock it behind me before walking down the hall to the elevator. The doors open on a ding right as I push the call button. This is clearly going to be my day!

I step off of the elevator and make my way through the lobby, wondering if I can make it to the station that is a few blocks away in time to make the train. I walk with a purpose, as my dad always says, and manage to make it through the turnstiles and to the track just in time to hop on the right train. I almost think I should buy a lottery ticket if this is how the rest of my day is going to go.

I step off the train at my stop and climb the stairs to the street level before making my way down the street to the animal shelter. I first found this shelter when I began volunteering with Purple Paws, an organization that takes dogs from shelters and trains them to pair with veterans in need of service dogs from PTSD to helper aids. When I was approached with the idea of an organization that takes two wounded souls and bonds them together for the greater good. I was hooked from day one. And then I met the lovely people who run this animal shelter when they aren't working for the vet clinic to the upper echelon of New York.

I push through the door with a lot of heavy thoughts swirling through my brain. Winks has been on my mind lately. A sweet-natured gray cat with a big, soulful green eye. The second was lost when someone used him as bait in a dog fight. Winks must have gotten away, but he was still pretty banged up when someone found him before bringing him here.

Stacy was going to check on him. The vets at the animal hospital say he's going to make it, but the animal shelter isn't so sure someone will adopt a one-eyed cat with a lot of emotional baggage. They've been hinting for a while now that when he is well enough to come home, it should be with me. And while I haven't admitted it out loud yet, I'm beginning to think they're right. I just haven't wanted to call him mine yet in case he made a turn for the worse. The wound from losing Pepper is still too raw and losing another furry friend so soon would cut deep. But the truth is, I'm already attached. Winks is mine and we all know it.

"Hey, Grace," Jamie, the girl working the front desk calls out. "Here to check on your boy or visit all the rest?"

"I'm here to check on my boy," I say, giving her a knowing look that she just laughs at. "How is he doing anyway?"

"Great," Stacy replies as she walks from the back. "He's going to be just fine and should be able to go home in a few days."

"That's fantastic news," I tell her.

"I thought you'd be happy about that one," she says. "So, are you finally going to admit you're adding him to the pack at your place?"

"Yes," I drawl. "Winks is mine and you all knew it, and so did I."

"Good," she says on a small smile. "He'll be right where he belongs."

I wave to her as she makes her way out of the building before I head on back to see Winks. He perks up when he sees me come into the back room, and I go right to his kennel. I pop the door open, and he stands up on shaky legs.

"Merow."

"Hey, buddy," I say to him as I gently scoop him up into my arms. "How's it going today?"

Winks just lets out a happy purr as I carry him into

the break room. There is a big comfy recliner that had come from someone's home, and I sit down in it with my new main man in my lap. Out of my bag, I pull a small throw blanket from my home that smells like me and all the other cats and curl it around us to see what he'll do, but I never should have worried. Winks settles down as if he knows he's found his pack.

"I have so much to tell you," I say in a calm voice. "I went to a gala last night. And I'm pretty sure we got a good foot in the door on the Open Arms project. There's just one problem."

The cat looks at me with his big, green eye as if he's really listening to me explain my problems. I think he just might be. It makes me feel better to think that someone might actually care what I have to say.

"Roughly one third of the backers I need will only support the project if I can get Senator Chancellor signed on as a sponsor. They think it will be good to have his name attached to the project for veterans, and I know they're right, but I just don't want to work with him. He's a stubborn jerk, and I know it will be just miserable working with him. He will boss me around and try to change all my plans and… and… and make me like him, and I just can't do that. It'll be all right without him, right?"

"Meow."

"Well who asked you?" Oh my gosh, I can't believe I'm talking man problems with a cat and he has the nerve to disagree with me. What the hell am I going to do? "I'll just stick to cats. Men always make things complicated. Cats don't talk back, right?"

"Meow."

I let out a sigh. "That's what I thought."

RUMORS OF A JEFFRIES-CHANCELLOR WEDDING FLY

THREE

The trap

Everything is going to be just fine.

I smooth down my pencil skirt and stand to greet Jules, one of my best friends from college, when the hostess leads her to the dark booth with crisp white linens in the back of one of New York's most exclusive restaurants.

Jules pulls me into a tight hug before removing her coat and handing it to the hostess to hang up outside our booth before sliding gracefully into her seat. Everything about Jules is posh and polished. Where I feel like a fraud, like a little girl playing dress up in her mother's fancy clothes, Julia Fairchild is the real deal.

I met her my freshman year of college when I rushed the sororities. She was also a freshman going through the recruitment process. She was a bright light when I was scared out of my mind. Naturally shy, I wasn't sure what I'd been thinking when I promised my mom I would try to make friends. This was so far outside my comfort zone that I never would have been there normally if I hadn't made a promise.

Jules was a legacy, meaning her mom and both grandmothers had also belonged to the same sorority. Her parents met because their mothers were sorority sisters. Jules knew exactly what sorority she was going to, and none of the overly loud parties, theme T-shirts, or silly songs about friendship and sisterhood scared her or put her off.

She also took one look at me in a sea of freshman women and knew with that one look I was in way over my head. So, in true Jules fashion, she decided that night we were going to be best friends. She ushered me through rush week and new member activities, and without her I probably would have hated college. Instead, I not only loved it, but I made lifelong friendships, Jules included. I love Jules like a sister, so I'm always happy she's free for our weekly drinks and dinner.

"So," she says excitedly. If anything, Jules loves life as well. "How are things going?"

I'm not, however, going to tell her that my project is about to sink like a stone. So I smile, open my mouth, and lie. "Things are great."

She eyes me seriously as the waiter approaches. "We'll get back to that in a minute."

"Hi, ladies, my name is Anthony," he greets on a

charming smile. "Can I get you anything to drink from the bar tonight?"

"Yes," Jules answers immediately as she eyes Anthony like a hungry lion. "We would both like dirty martinis, extra dirty, extra olives, and blue cheese olives at that."

"Sounds great," he says. "Anything else?"

"A charcuterie board when you get a chance, and keep the vodka coming. I have a feeling we're going to need it."

I feel my lips press into a tight line as she speaks. I should have known I couldn't keep anything from Jules. She always could read me like a book.

"Coming right up."

"So—" She turns her focus to me after Anthony walks away. "—have you talked to Angie lately?"

"Not recently," I reply. "Last I heard, she was deep in wedded bliss with Cody in some small town in Texas." Angie, our third friend, left New York when she found her boyfriend banging a nurse at the hospital they both worked at. Her aunt whisked her off to a small town in East Texas, where she fell in love with a retired professional football player. I have a feeling there will be a whole sea of little football-loving babies before long. Their brand-new daughter, Joy, is a fantastic start.

"That's what I hear," Jules agrees on a sigh. "I miss her though."

"Me too. And Aunt Mable."

Jules smiles at that. "She was always worse than the three of us."

"I hear nothing's changed on that front."

"Here you go, ladies," Anthony says as he places a cold martini glass in front of each of us and a wooden carving board of breads, cheeses, and fruits between us.

"Thank you," I say on a smile as I reach for my glass.

Jules, again, turns her attention back to me as he walks away, and my sip turns into a gulp. I know her inquisition is coming; I just don't want to answer right now.

"So, now, what's really going on?" she asks me.

"Why would you think anything is going on?" I counter her question with one of my own.

"Because you are evading my question, and you never do that unless something is bothering you, so you might as well just spit it out. I'm going to find out anyway."

"That's true," I say on a sigh.

"So, what is it?" Jules asks as she serves up bread and cheese on two small plates before passing me one.

"My Open Arms project is dead in the water," I admit before stuffing a giant bite of bread in my mouth. Sometimes you just have to admit to yourself that life kind of sucks in the moment and then eat your feelings.

I'm okay with accepting that now is my moment.

"Why would you say that?"

"Last night, I went to the gala for Purple Paws, and Senator Chancellor was there," I begin to explain.

"And how is the man of the hour?" she asks. "I hear his campaign is off and running."

"Ruining my life," I snap a little too harshly before regretting my misplaced emotion in a public setting. I reach for my glass again and take another huge sip.

"Easy there, killer." She smirks. "So how is Bachelor of the Year ruining your life? Tell Auntie Julia, so she can fix it and make the mean man pay."

"Don't be ridiculous," I say as I take my time spreading a soft cheese over a piece of bread. "Every single person I talked to about backing my project said they would only commit if Chancellor was connected."

"Every single one? That seems a bit excessive."

"It was. Everyone wants him or access to him," I whine.

"He *is* running for President of the United States," she says softly before sipping her cocktail. "I can understand why people are interested."

"But my project?" I ask. "I don't need him."

"One could argue at this juncture that you do," she tells me quietly just before Anthony comes back to take our dinner order and deliver another martini to me.

"Don't remind me!" I practically whine. God, I hate who he makes me be. I am not this whiny person.

I don't need him to clear the path for me, dammit. I will clear it on my own.

"What can I get you ladies?" Anthony asks.

"The steak, medium, baked potato, and a salad," she orders.

"Very good," he says before turning to me. "And for you?"

By now, I'm a fair amount of vodka and not a lot of food deep, something I never do, so I follow Jules's lead and load up. "The same for me please."

"Now tell me why we don't like the sexy senator again?" she says.

"He's just so… so…" I stammer. There is too much vodka swirling around in my brain to avoid words like sexy or tantalizing. How can I explain that I can't be near him without falling onto his penis which is, no doubt, always ready, and I also can't stand to watch other women receive the pleasure of his company. And I'm sure there is plenty of pleasure to go around where Jake Chancellor is concerned.

"So, what?" she prods with an unattractive smirk playing around her mouth. She twirls her glass by the stem while she watches me. It's really unfortunate when someone knows you so well that they have all of your tells memorized. I know that she knows that I'm full of bullshit. A real friend wouldn't mention, but Jules is the best so I know she's about to call me on it.

"Frustrating."

"I hear he's good at scratching that particular itch too," she adds with a wicked smile on her face.

"Not funny." I toss back the rest of my martini before slicing another piece of cheese and shoving it in my mouth. I love a cheese board. I even make them in the quiet of my own apartment to enjoy while I binge hallmark movies with my cats. I realize now that makes me sound pathetic.

"I thought it was particularly," she adds, not at all helpful.

"I don't want to watch him parade around all of his… groupies and their sordid tales. I just want to build the Open Arms Center and move on to the next project."

"Could you maybe be a bit jealous of the groupies?" she asks me, honing in on my exact problem. I am jealous. I don't want to watch the parade of his lady of the moment one after another, because he would never choose me, and if he did, it would only be for a night, and that would cut way too deep. I'm strong and firmly self-sufficient, but I'm so attracted to Chancellor that the sting of his rejection would burn too much. And when faced with these truths, I wonder if maybe he's not as bad as I have always told myself, maybe if given half the chance, I could care for him and that would be even worse.

"Of course not!"

"Me thinks the lady doth protest too much," she says as she delicately sips her drink while mine is once again, long gone.

"I do not," I say adamantly. I will go down with this ship of denial at this point, even if it kills me.

"Then you'll be happy to know the gentleman in question is sitting right up front," she shares, nodding her head to the front of the room behind me.

"What?" I squeak and nearly choke on an olive.

"Maybe you should go talk to him, break the ice," she suggests not at all helpfully.

"Absolutely not."

And thankfully, I am saved by Anthony bringing our dinner to the table so I do not have to argue with Jules any more about Jake Chancellor or anyone else.

"MAYBE WE SHOULD PLAN a trip to go visit Angie," she says after we've settled the check and are preparing to part ways for another two weeks.

"I would love that. Let's do it. Maybe after the holidays?"

"Let's plan it," she says as she pulls me into a tight hug. "And I really think he's not the bad guy you've made him out to be in your head."

I shoot her the side-eye. "I think you've lost your mind. That man has dangerous written all over him."

"Hmm," she hums. "I never said dangerous can't be fun."

"But it's also not me," I tell her and that's the absolute truth. I'm a play it safe kind of a gal. I've never been one to leap off a cliff and hope the soft waves below catch me. Maybe that's why Chancellor bothers me so much. He's wild and dangerous, like a leopard and I'm nothing but an old house cat. He would be bored with me before the first day was over.

"That's true," she says thoughtfully. "Just see what he has to offer."

"Fine. I'll call his office in the morning," I promise. I can do that. I'll talk to an aid in his office and find out if he's interested in collaborating. All while hoping that he absolutely does not.

"Fabulous." She smiles. "Then call me and tell me everything."

"I will," I promise, leaning in to hug her again. The thought of a trip with Jules and Angie is perfect, just what I need to set my world right again. I didn't realize how much I had missed Angie now that she lives halfway across the world until Jules had mentioned seeing her again.

"I'll talk to you soon," she says, and then she's gone.

I slide my coat on but don't button it up. It's too hot in the restaurant, so I leave it open and pick up my clutch. I start walking toward the front door, and that's when I spot him sitting casually as if he hasn't a care in the world, sipping a glass of his signature scotch. Everyone knows the Senator loves a glass on the rocks from time to time, but like me, he never overindulges.

What are the odds that the man who has been driving me crazy is here in the very same restaurant tonight? For a second, I let myself wonder what it would be like if things were different. What if he wasn't with a different woman every time he steps out in public? What if he really was interested in me? But like I always knew, that's too many what ifs.

His two Secret Service agents stand back against the wall, but you could still spot them anywhere. They are anything but covert. I wonder if he ever forgets they are there. Or what they must have heard or seen in their time in service with him. I guess it's all part of being a United States Senator, and if he is elected to the highest office, there will only be more restrictions on him, more agents to protect him.

For the first time, I admit that maybe his life isn't so easy after all. Or maybe that's just the three martinis talking.

I watch him slip his phone from his pocket and fire off a text to someone before the waiter brings him a fresh drink. I shake my head to clear the unhealthy thoughts—and any thoughts of Jake Chancellor being a nice guy are unhealthy.

I start to make my way through the restaurant again when someone from last night stops me to ask me about the Open Arms project.

"Grace," he says, breaking me free from my thoughts. "Just who I was talking about."

"How are you this evening?" I ask politely and wave at the men he is dining with. These are all prominent businessmen in New York, and I need them and their money to get this project off the ground.

"Good, good," they answer. "We were just wondering if you've given any more thought to bringing the senator on board?"

I barely hold in my sigh of frustration and smile. Seriously? It's only been a day since we spoke, and they want me to abandon all my plans and heel to a certain senator who drives me crazy. But this is my life, this is the life I have built for myself, and I am not going to let anyone—even Jacob Chancellor—chase me away from it. So, I square my shoulders and answer them. "It's under consideration."

"Do consider it," one of the men says firmly. "I won't sign on without him."

"I do hope we can all come to an agreement on this," another states.

"I think time will tell," I say, trying to extricate myself for this conversation. "Now if you'll excuse me, it's getting late."

I move closer and closer to him and hold my breath. I'm hoping he doesn't notice me and I can move on without being seen.

"You've got my vote," I overhear the waiter saying to Chancellor.

"Thank you," he replies, and it seems genuine. "That means a lot to me."

I'm almost to his table now when another prominent businessman stops me to ask about the man at the very top of my "I don't want to talk about it" list. I feel my frustration at my escape plans being foiled again pull across my face, but I halt it in its tracks. It's only for a second before I quickly school my features into a serene expression. I'm a fucking professional after all. I really hope he doesn't notice me.

But when I look over my shoulder again, I'm not so lucky. The Senator is watching me with open, unguarded interest. He pushes his seat back ever so slightly from the table he is sitting at as if he's going to stand and greet me like we're old friends. I know for a fact that he would like to be more than friends, but I'm just not willing to risk it.

I was planning to keep my focus straight ahead, even if it is more than a little rude, and ignore Jake Chancellor, when the sole of one of my ridiculously tall Louboutins steps on a spoon that someone haphazardly dropped on the floor, and I begin to slide like an ice skater. I recover, or I try to, but the slight tipping of my body tells a different story. I slowly start to tip backward, but Chancellor is right there. He stands up from his chair and catches me as I finally lose my balance. He pulls my body tight to his.

His right palm lands flat on my ass cheek and burns

me through my dress. We both feel a shiver wrack up my spine, and I jerk my body back, but he doesn't let go of me while his left hand goes to the back of my neck. His fingers slide into the thick mass of my hair, and I love the feel of it there, pulling ever so slightly, more than I ever could have imagined. His face goes into the side of my neck and I barely restrain the rough groan that almost slips from my lips. My head tips back and my eyes slide closed.

"Are you all right?" he asks after longer than he should have waited to check on me, to release me. He whispers the words in my ear in deliciously low tones, so those at the tables around us can't hear.

"Y-y-yes," I stammer softly.

He tips his head back and gets a good look at my face. The slight move has me pressing my waist into his impressive erection. I should have known he'd be huge. The world is so unfair, but in this moment, I don't care. I'm lost. I'm sure my cheeks are flushed a bright pink from my embarrassment. My eyes are bright with… lust? I just don't know what this feeling is or what I should do with it. And I might be mistaken, but I'm pretty sure my nipples are hard peaks pressed against his dress-shirt-clad chest.

Now that is unfortunate.

"You can unhand me now," I say quietly, but I pack enough steel into my voice—the voice I use in the courtroom—to let him know that playtime is over. For now.

"Of course," he replies, letting me hear the interest in his tone. "I'm happy to catch you any time."

"I'm sure you are," I tell him with a smirk playing on my lips. I can't help but hope he doesn't notice I have only taken one tiny step back from him.

"I'm all too happy to be at your service any time," he adds, smiling his most charming smile, with those stupid dimples and all, and I try hard not to notice that with me it seems more natural and less forced. "All you have to do is call."

"We shall see, Senator," I say. "Have a good night."

"You too, Grace."

And then I slip by him and walk out into the night. I have the valet hail me a cab, and then I'm gone.

But what I didn't know then was that I wouldn't be gone for long. Later, I would wish I had noticed the plethora of camera flashes that shot all around us from the second I landed in his arms until the cab door closed behind me and I rolled away into the New York night.

I spent the cab ride back to my apartment still feeling his strong arms around me and his calloused hand on my ass. I played the look of his face over and over in my head, wondering as I did at the time if he was thinking about kissing me like I had thought about kissing him. What I did not feel was a steel cage closing around me. Oh, by tomorrow afternoon, the game would change. I was well and truly caught. I just didn't know how.

The trap had been set.

SEXY SENATOR SPOTTED WITH MYSTERY WOMAN.

FOUR

Work, work, work... oh crap

Today is going to be a beautiful day!

I reach over to my nightstand and pick up my phone. I slide my finger up the screen to silence my alarm. I'm probably one of very few people who don't hate Mondays. Mondays are a great start to the week. I like to see my schedule all plotted out and planned. My secretary is a god among men, and what he can do with a spreadsheet and a calendar reminds me that the rest of us are just mere mortals. I'm truly lost without him. Luckily for me, I don't have to be.

Also, Carter sees the mission of the greater good. He loves all the cloak-and-dagger shit that goes with running a secret legal aid society using the money I make from our high-profile clients, not to mention Jules kicks in a bunch of her old family money when no one is looking while she rules the air waves as one of the nation's leading anchors for Eagle News Network. He has likened us to Clark Kent and Lois Lane. I'm Clark.

The silly code names Carter has monikered for us always make me smile, and that is exactly what I'm doing now as I throw back the covers and make my way into the kitchen to feed my tiny furry army. All eight of my little loves hustle into the kitchen and wait in their spots for breakfast when they hear the telltale signs of me moving in the morning. I turn my Keurig on before I pull their bowls from the cabinet and dish up their grub. Everyone is silent this morning as we are back to our early morning routine.

I quickly brew a cup of coffee and make my way back to my bathroom to get ready for the day. I strip off my pajamas and turn the taps in my shower to heat up the water before stepping into the tub with my coffee cup in hand. Time is of the essence!

By the time I finish washing, my coffee is also gone. I turn off the water and grab a towel. I wrap it around my body while I brush and dry my hair with a round brush before styling it in a sleek ballet bun on top of my head. I hang my towel back up on the rack before brushing my teeth and applying a light amount of makeup for a classic look. I smile at myself in the mirror. Last night, Jules helped me realize I need to put my personal feelings for Senator Chancellor aside and do the right thing for Open Arms. And it does feel right. After work, I'm going to contact his office and ask them to put my project on his desk.

I make my way into my closet and suit up in my uniform of the day—Chanel and Louboutin. I put a classic watch on my wrist and small diamond studs in my ears before heading out for the day. Again, the elevator arrives with a ding as I hit the call button, and when I step out the front door of my building, a cab magically appears as soon as I lift my hand in the air in that age-old signal that is bred into all New Yorkers.

Today is going to be an amazing day!

I FEEL LIKE THAT Rhianna song—work, work, work. All day long, Carter and I move through our schedule of one high-powered client after the next, solving problems as we go. I kind of feel a little unstoppable today. I have that gut feeling everything is about to work out just the way it's supposed to, even though on my way uptown this morning there was another cache of tabloids all featuring Senator Chancellor splashed all over them. But then again, there's nothing new there. Every morning, titles like "Jake's Big Snake Tell-All" or "My Night in the Sexy Senator's Bed" grace the front pages of every publication.

Jules even has to cover him often, as her job as a

major cable news anchor requires it. Thankfully, Jules is a class act. She only covers the election and his work as a U.S. Senator. She wouldn't lower herself to common gossip.

I've just finished with another client in the conference room and am heading back to my corner office when Carter stops me in the hallway.

"Hey, Clark," he calls out, making me smile.

"What's up, Carter?"

"I need your lunch order for the deli," he says. "And this was left on my desk for you."

"That spinach and berry salad that I can't seem to stay away from. With some grilled chicken please. And what's this?" I ask as I take the plain manila envelope from his hands.

"I have no idea," he says with a shrug. "I should have lunch in your office in thirty."

"Sounds good. Thanks." I make my way back into my office and shut the door behind me. I drop the envelope on top of my desk and sit down in my chair. My feet ache from my power shoes, but I don't care. The pain keeps me aware of my surroundings, and right now my Spidey senses are dinging away as I stare at the sealed envelope in front of me.

I carefully pick it up. It doesn't feel very heavy. I take a deep breath and roll my shoulders back. It's probably nothing. But it doesn't feel like nothing. I slide a delicately polished fingernail under the seal and lift the flap. I pull out a single sheet of paper with a short, typed note on it and find I was right all along; this isn't nothing. This is bad. It's so very bad.

Today is not amazing!

"No. No, no, no, no, no!" I say as I shake the envelope and a stack of glossy pictures falls out on top of the note. I can already see what they're of, and it doesn't surprise me like it should. I can still feel his hand burning its imprint onto the skin of my ass. One look at my face and my arousal is there for all to see, not to mention the outline of my hard nipples pressing against the silk of my favorite little black dress. My worst fears have been imagined. It looks like last night I accidentally became another notch in the bedpost of Jacob Monroe Chancellor, and all because of a carelessly dropped dessert spoon.

He looks like he wanted *you* for dessert.

This can't be happening. My hands shake as I flip through picture after picture. How could this have happened? I've been so careful. I have meticulously watched every move I have ever made throughout my entire life. I never drink too much or eat too much. I have never partaken in recreational pharmaceuticals or otherwise. I don't stay out late and party. And every lover I've ever had has been not only respectable but also discrete—*hell, the last two signed Non-Disclosure Agreements*—and if I'm being honest, a little boring. Actually, my life is more than a little boring. So boring that I just don't know how this could have even happened.

My heart is beating so fast in my chest I feel like I

might be sick. Drops of sweat are trickling down from my temples and between my breasts, and my skin is flushed hot. And not in a good way. Not in the way it flushed last night when the sexy senator gripped my ass in his strong hand like a man who knew what he wanted to do with it. And for a split second last night, I wanted him like I have never wanted a man before. Crap.

But anyone looking in the windows of my palatial corner office would see exactly what I want them to. This is what I show the world every day, that I am calm, cool, and collected. I am the master of my world. I keep myself poised and in control no matter what. I don't play around. I have worked way too hard for my career. My reputation precedes me all over town—and *this* town is an important one.

I let the stack of glossy drug store one-hour prints fall on top of the plain manila envelope they came in, where it sits on top of my mahogany desk. In secret, I call it my fancy desk. It was my dad's desk in his office at his own law firm, and when I was a little girl, I used to say the ornate carvings on the front were "fancy." It sits proud with its elegant scroll work along the edges.

I didn't grow up like this. My parents are respected attorneys here in New York, but I made the family name a commodity in high-power circles where they need me and desperately want to know me.

I recoil from the envelope as if it's a rattlesnake sitting on my desk and not the stack of worthless paper that it is. But my conscience whispers that it's not worthless. This envelope of pictures could be *very* valuable in the right—or should I say wrong—hands. There are plenty of people here in New York who would just love to get their hands on this caliber of ammunition to use against me.

This package was sent to my office by courier with my name type-printed on the front and a note inside written in thick, block letters.

I'LL BE IN TOUCH.
DON'T SAY A WORD.

I'm sure if I took it to the police, there would be no fingerprints either. But I can't do that anyway. If I go to the police, this will be all over town and it will ruin my reputation. I am the attorney no one can touch. I am who the powerful go to when they need someone to pull their fat out of the fryer, and I have worked very hard to become that person. I trade in power and money every day behind closed doors and use those commodities to secretly help those who would never be able to help themselves—the poor and downtrodden. I'm like the freaking Statue of Liberty herself, and this mess has the potential to ruin everything. How ironic that my carefully crafted house of cards is about to come down with a few pictures of me in the arms of a well-known man.

The worst part: I didn't even do it. Sure, he held me for a minute. Probably longer than he should have, but I tripped. That was it. And now it's going to ruin everything.

I tap the red-painted sole of my black patent leather Louboutins on the carpet. It's the only outward sign of my distress, and I keep that shit thoroughly hidden behind my desk. Now the question is, how do I proceed? I need to figure out what to do to keep my world from crashing down and fast.

I pick up my cellphone—the latest model that hasn't even been announced yet—and slide my carefully manicured index finger up the dark glass. It scans my face and unlocks. I scroll through my contacts until I see the one I don't want to dial with every fiber of my being. I could laugh, because four hours ago, I was planning on reaching out to his people for an all-too-different reason. I stare it down like it's a bomb ticking down on the clock every second before it explodes in my face—just like I know this decision will later—before I finally force myself to take a deep breath and hit the Call button.

"Hello?" a whiskey-smooth voice answers. I hate that the sound of him makes me furious and my panties wet. This is definitely an unwelcome predicament.

"I need your help," I say. The words taste like sawdust on my tongue and acid churns in my belly.

"What an interesting turn of events," he replies, and I hate how damn happy he sounds. As if my fall from greatness is something to be celebrated. Of course, he doesn't know my life is hanging precariously in the balance. How could he?

"Don't sound so smug," I warn my adversary. "This affects you as much as it does me."

"Like I said—*interesting*. Meet me at the Magic Boarding House Tavern at eight o'clock," he says. "I'll be waiting."

I open my mouth to issue a witty putdown, but I'm too late. A dial sound goes off in my ear, letting me know that slimeball hung up on me. I want to scream. Everything is hanging by a thread, and I don't even know how I can combat this. Clearly, the person who sent the pictures wants something from me. I just don't know what. And why didn't they just tell me straight out? Why make me wait?

My only hope now is that he can get me out of this mess. I know it's going to cost me; I just hope it's a price I'm able to live with. And also that I can stay strong and resist a certain U.S. Senator with less than questionable morals and his stupid dimples, because sex and blackmail certainly don't mix, but in reality, I'm more than screwed.

I TOOK A CHANCE
ON CHANCELLOR'S
MAGIC STICK.

FIVE

Hope is nothing but a bunch of bullshit.

I should have known better. I was surprised when Chancellor suggested a place as innocuous as the Magic Boarding House, a favorite haunt for gamer nerds from all over the world. It features a large game store where people can play or buy hard-to-find games. And it also has a dark tavern where anyone can grab a bite to eat. My mistake was in assuming that a place as family friendly as this one wouldn't be the setting for my epic fall from grace. But now, as I move toward the back of the tavern part of the boarding house, I spy him sitting at a booth in the far back corner, shuffling a deck of cards like he grew up in the back room of an Atlantic City casino—which, to my knowledge, he did not. And I know I made a mistake. I shouldn't have underestimated him and let my guard down.

I was surprised when he asked me to meet him here, but then again, any of my regular haunts would be absolutely packed with people we know or who want to know us, and we are here to solve our mutual problem with the press.

I watch as he tips his wrist back to look at the Tag Heuer watch on his arm to check the time. It's ten minutes to eight, and I am early. I'd wanted to get here first to establish territory and gain the upper hand, but it looks like the senator beat me at my own game.

He slides out from the booth and smiles as he notices me approaching his table with a rueful smile playing on my lips at his power move. I teeter a little in my sky-high heels when he flashes me those panty-melting dimples. I still wore my signature Louboutins, because they make me feel powerful, and I *am* powerful, but I have replaced my Chanel suit with a pair of dark jeans and a dove-gray silk blouse with a matching dove-gray leather jacket over it. He looks at me like I think the Big Bad Wolf looked at Little Red Riding Hood, and I swallow back a nervous laugh that threatens to bubble up to the surface.

I need to keep my mind in the game in order to win this round with Senator Chancellor.

"Hello, Grace," he says as he leans in and places a sweet kiss on my cheek before motioning toward the booth. "Have a seat."

"Hello, Senator Chancellor," I reply as I slip my

jacket from my shoulders and place it on the bench seat beside me with my purse on top of it after I slide in. I toy with the small folded menu in front of me instead of meeting the watchful gaze of the man seated across from me. He makes me nervous and I don't know why—or I do know why, but I'm refusing to put words to the emotions he stirs in me. This shy schoolgirl isn't me. I am a "take life by the balls and forge my own path" kind of a woman, and it's time she showed up to the party.

"Have you ever been here before?" he asks me, and I finally look up at his handsome face.

"No," I reply softly. "Have you?"

He smiles what I can only assume is a genuine smile, because it's not one I see on him often, before he answers me. "I meet friends here at least once a month."

The look on my face must show my surprise at his answer, because he throws his head back and laughs. It's one of the nicest sounds I have ever heard, and watching his whole face light up like that while the always-ready posture of his body relaxes just a tiny bit is one of the sexiest I have ever seen. It's in this moment that I know I could give in to him and it would be amazing. But just as amazing as it would be, I also know it would be devastating.

"I do have friends, you know," he says with a smile.

"You do?" I question as I try to pose my face in a faux-shocked expression.

"I do." He smiles so that his twin dimples wink at me like stars glittering in the sky. Good Lord, there is something about this man. There's just… more to him and I can't help but want it even though I shouldn't.

"Who?" I continue to play along, and the banter is so easy and fun that part of me wonders why I have kept him at arm's length for years. Why haven't I given in to this pull between us?

"Rick, for one—" he starts to answer.

"And where is your delightful henchman tonight?" I ask, blinking my eyes innocently.

"One, Rick isn't that bad," he manages to say with a straight face.

"He really is," I say on a laugh. Clearly, their friendship has desensitized him to his friend's evil political deeds as his campaign mercenary.

"There's more to Rick than meets the eye," he says cryptically.

"Of that, I am absolutely sure of."

"And two, I'm allowed to go out without him from time to time," he adds. I look over his shoulder and see two of his regular Secret Service agents standing with their backs against the wall, watching for anyone who might want to do the senator harm. He might be allowed to go out without Rick Donovan from time to time, but he isn't allowed to go anywhere alone. Ever. That thought makes me feel kind of sad for him.

"I suppose you are," I tell him softly. "I bet you're

a heavily sought-after man."

"I am," he sighs.

"And you come here to unwind?" I surmise.

"I do. Rick and I have been meeting friends here for a while now," he answers honestly.

"You mean women." I laugh when he rolls his eyes. "What? You know you're popular—"

"No, we do not meet women here," he says in a rather disgruntled fashion. "The Magic Boarding House Tavern is sacred and not to be defiled."

"So, you come here to what? Play Magic?" I ask incredulously.

"Yes, I do," he responds to my question, mirroring my wide stare with one of his own.

"With Rick?" Somehow, I can't picture the most feared man in politics playing a nerdy card game with friends. The idea of him in a relaxed environment is jarring. Like two puzzle pieces that don't quite fit together.

"With Rick and sometimes Wes and Lee, but not Wes so much, because he recently got married and likes to stay close to home," he explains.

"And you don't like that?"

"No, I'm happy for him. Claire is a great woman. We should all be so lucky, and after she almost died last year," he explains, "I would stay close to her and home if she were mine too."

"You don't mean Claire Goodnite—the detective

from New Jersey who was kidnapped as a young girl?" I ask.

"The one and only."

"Wow, I read about her in the *Post* last year. You really know her?"

"Yeah, her brother and her husband are friends of mine," he explains. "We served together on the same team when we were in the Navy."

"Wow." I knew Chancellor had served as a Navy SEAL, but I didn't know he was also connected to local heroes as well. I guess I should have paid more attention to him instead of just running for the hills every time he walked into a room.

"So, you said you have a problem…." He trails off, breaking me free from my wayward thoughts. This is good. I need him to help me stay focused so I can solve my problem and move on with my life. Then Jake Chancellor and his magic penis won't be a threat to me anymore, because I'll be hiding in some remote village in South America and he will be fully entrenched in the Oval Office. Then I can come back to New York and forget this whole time in my life ever happened, right?

I let out a frustrated sigh before brushing back a blonde curl that has fallen out of place across my forehead. I look at him again, sitting across the table from me. He's looking back at me like he thinks I'm adorable like a little kitten. But this kitten will kill you in your sleep if you're not careful. So he better watch out. I won't pull any punches with him.

"Grace?" he asks when I still don't answer.

I push out another uneasy breath and force myself to respond to his early question. "Yeah, Senator. I have a problem."

"Well, it can't be that bad," he hedges. It's as if he can't even fathom the idea I could be in as much trouble as I currently am.

"It is."

"And it involves me?" he asks.

"Yeah."

"Care to explain?"

I really don't want to answer him. God, if only I could go to bed and when I wake up in the morning it would all be a bad dream. But this is a dream I can't wake up from. This nightmare is my real life.

"I wish I didn't have to," I say cryptically. I roll my bottom lip into my mouth and bite down hard.

"Go on."

"Just…" I toss a manila envelope on the table in front of him. "Here."

He stares at the package in front of him before reaching for it. Chancellor flips back the flap and peers inside. He couldn't possibly know what's in there. That his career and mine are about to take a major hit. And then he reaches in and pulls out a stack of pictures. He flips through them and thoroughly investigates each picture of me and himself in a pretty sexy clinch. Each image is hotter than the next. I barely resist the urge to squirm in my seat just thinking of how we look together like that.

"Well." He forces out the words before clearing his throat and shifting a little in his seat. I know how he feels. The pictures are…moving, to say the least. "Those are some pictures."

"And the note," I add.

Chancellor looks back in the envelope and pulls out a single piece of computer paper with a handwritten note on it. He looks up at me with questions in his eyes, and believe me, I have them too. But I don't have any answers for either of us. How I wish I had answers.

"That's all?" he asks. "They didn't make any demands?"

"Not yet," I tell him. "I think they're going to use this to ruin me."

"Ruin you?" he asks. "How?"

"My reputation is flawless," I explain. I'm not wrong, and we both know it.

"It is."

"My reputation is how I sway juries and fix the problems of powerful people," I tell him. "If that reputation is ruined, I have nothing." And I will never let that happen. I would burn everything to the ground before I let some nameless asshole take everything I have worked so hard for from me. It depends on how things unfold from here on out.

"And you think this… person wants to ruin you?"

he asks again. "For what goal?"

"I have some pretty big cases coming up."

"Like what?"

I shoot him an incredulous look. He should know better than to ask me such a stupid question. Of course I can't tell him. And especially not in such a public setting.

"You know I can't answer that."

"True, I figured it never hurts to try," he says with a shrug. "And how do you think these pictures could… ruin you?" Just hearing the words is like a punch to the gut.

"Those pictures don't paint a pretty picture," I say by way of an explanation. I don't want him to know how real the look on my face is in those pictures.

"They're sexy as hell, I'll give you that," he tells me the truth as I look at them again. I kind of want to keep one for my own personal viewing, but that feels a little dirty. For him, I know I could be dirty. "But how could it ruin you?"

I sit across from him and look at him for a long while. Why doesn't he understand how serious this is? Is he not taking me seriously on purpose? How can I make him see reason?

"I can't be seen as another notch in your bedpost," I finally reply in such a quiet voice that he can barely hear me. "No one will ever take me seriously again. And I don't know how to fix it. I need your help, and I absolutely hate everything about that."

"Lucky for you I have an idea," he says as he watches me to gauge my reaction, and I hope he fucking does have an answer, because I feel like I'm drowning without a life jacket.

"And what would that be?" I ask. "I'm all ears."

"You marry me, of course."

I had just reached for the water glass in front of me and taken a sip when he told me that his answer to all of my problems was to marry the king of the alley cats, the man who has had a record amount of bedmates and couldn't possibly be faithful to someone as boring as me. The mouthful of water I just took, I spit all across the table and all over him.

"W-w-what?" I stammer.

"I'm not into spit play, sweetheart, but I can come up with something you'll like a whole lot more. I promise," he says to me with a straight face as he reaches for the napkin in front of him and pats his face dry.

"Explain yourself right now," I demand.

"I'd much prefer you swallow," Chancellor adds with a devious smirk playing at the corner of his mouth. He is obviously being obtuse in an effort to be cute or flirty, and I just can't handle that right now. I need clear facts and straight talk right now.

"That's not what I'm talking about and you know it."

"If we come out as a serious couple and eventually

get engaged, no one will see you as another woman in my bed. You will be the only woman in my bed," he explains.

"No one will believe it," I rationalize. This is what I need. I need to hash out the details and come up with a clear plan. What I do not need is to marry a man who could never love me, just for the sake of looks. "A woman just sold more pictures of you the other day. We can't get engaged right now. Everyone will think that I'm pregnant."

And now it's his turn to choke on the sip of water he just swallowed, obviously because the idea of having a baby with me is abhorrent. *Way to make a girl feel good about herself, Senator.*

"We've known each other for years," he rallies. "We'll tell people we've been circling around our attraction for years and we only just finally decided to give into it, but the feelings are real. We are very real."

"Maybe," I say. I don't want to see the logic of his crazy-ass plan. He looks like he can feel the win coming, and I cannot stand it. This can't be it. My whole life can't boil down to a political match that neither of us ever wanted. I have to find a way out of this predicament before Jake Chancellor talks me out of my panties and my pride.

"After a short while, we will get engaged, and by then the press will eat it up with a spoon. You'll be the darling of New York again."

"And then what?" I ask. I feel the hope that is shining in my eyes, and I pray I can find my way out of this mess before it's too late. I can "date" him for a while and show the world he's a reformed rake and I'm not just another notch in his bedpost. It'll all be fake—for show—obviously, and then he'll go on to win his election, because even though he's a tom cat on the prowl, he's also a great politician and the people love him. The polls show it. I just have to get through this, and then I can go back to my quiet life with my cats.

"And then we get married and win a presidential election," he explains, effectively crushing my hope. Why would he want to get married? That's utterly ridiculous.

"We can't possibly get married," I say for lack of anything else.

"And why is that?" Chancellor counters. "People of our station get married all the time for political reasons."

"You sound like a historical romance novel," I inform him. "'People of our station.' Who talks like that?"

"I do. And it's true. It's not like I don't admire you. I find you smart and driven, not to mention beautiful," he says. "I know you turn me on and so do you, because you felt how hard I was last night when you were pressed up against me."

I can't help the gasp that slips from my lips at his crude words, but I pull myself together as best as I can.

"A mild breeze would probably make you hard," I

tell him as I roll my eyes.

"Ouch!" He puts a hand to his chest. "You wound me."

"I think you'll survive," I droll.

"So you don't find me attractive?" he counters my argument.

"I never said that." And I do my best to bury the excitement I feel when bantering with Jake Chancellor as deep as I possibly can, because the temptation of giving in to him is oh so tempting.

"And I don't turn you on?" he asks me. "Because from here it looks like your nipples were hard little points in that tiny black dress, and I felt them against me."

"It was cold," I say, looking away from him as my cheeks turn pink. I don't want to give him any possible indication I might want him like he says he wants me. But I have a sinking feeling in the pit of my stomach that not much gets by Jake Chancellor.

"And there was that pretty pink blush," he explains as he points to his own cheeks. "Here." And then he points to the base of his neck. "And here. I can't help but wonder if you blush like that all over."

"Jacob." My voice is rough, and my eyes close as I try to shut out his words. I can't let them affect me like they do.

"You can call me Jake," he tells me. "Everyone else does."

"I think I prefer Jacob," I answer, and in that moment, he looks like he does too.

"What will you call me late at night?" he asks me after a moment, and his voice is husky and sultry. I know instinctively that this is how *he* sounds late at night, in bed after hours with a woman.

"Jacob."

"And what will you call me in bed?" he furthers.

"Jacob," I breathe, and I can feel myself giving in to him. He knows it, and so do I, but still… "I haven't agreed yet."

"But you will," he predicts. "What other choice do you have? Besides, imagine what you could do to change the world as First Lady."

"That is alarmingly tempting," I concede, but if I take up his offer to make me his First Lady, I will be doing it for all the wrong reasons. I could change the world, yes; we both know that I'm capable of anything. But without love, would it even matter? "Somehow, I bet you could tempt the devil himself."

"I don't want to tempt the devil. I just want to tempt you."

I look back at him, because his words, spoken quietly and without a hidden agenda, ring truer than anything else said tonight between us.

"And I like that you call me Jacob."

"And what happens when someone else sells a story from your bed when you're supposed to be hopelessly in love with me?" I ask, and I can't help but feel like a fool for looking more than a little vulnerable as I speak the question. I can't believe I let it slip that his affairs would bother me so much. I can only hope he reads my reluctance as worry over our image and not that his extramarital affairs would cut me deep when we're not even in a relationship to begin with. It all sounds so silly.

"There won't be any other women in my bed." His voice is strong and sure. He sounds so confident in himself and his ability to be faithful to a marriage with no love or intimacy.

"Why?" I blurt out before I can stop myself. I really should be more mindful of my words, but around Jacob Chancellor, I just can't seem to help myself.

"Because *you'll* be in my bed."

"You can't mean—" I start. I open and close my mouth a few times, but that seems to be all I can get out. He has me totally stunned.

"I do," he answers me calmly. It feels like he's thought about all of this before, but that can't be. He couldn't have known about the blackmail pictures before today. I know he's wanted me in his bed for a while now, but I had always assumed he wanted me there for a night or two, not installed in it for the rest of my life.

"But why?"

"Because I want you," he explains. "And because we're going to be a couple. When I marry you, there won't be anyone else in our marriage but us, regardless of how it came to be."

"Are you ready to order now?" the waiter asks.

"Grace?" Jacob prompts.

"How is the hummus basket?" I ask after clearing my throat.

"Freaking fantastic," he answers, making the waiter smile.

"And the buffalo wings?"

"Also amazing."

"Care to split them with me?" I need carbs and junk food in order to process the drastic left turn my life seems to have just taken.

"I'd love to." He smiles back at me before turning to the waiter. "The wings sampler and the hummus basket please."

"Got it," he says. "Anything to drink for you guys?" And this must be why he likes to come here. No one stands on ceremony for him here. He is just like everyone else.

"The IPA," I answer.

"Me too, please."

"Coming right up."

"Maybe we won't need to get married," I say hesitantly when he walks away. "Maybe the dust will blow over and we can consciously uncouple like the celebrities do and still see you settled in the White House."

"Sure," he replies, but the way he says it is more

like "Not a fucking chance in hell."

I eye him warily, and I can't help but wonder if he has even more nefarious motives than trying to fuck me while I repair my reputation.

"Now, let's talk details," he says, sitting back in his seat and making himself more comfortable. He's clearly at ease here, and that puts me firmly on my guard.

"What about the details? We go on a few fake dates, maybe give a press release, right?"

"Here's your IPAs," the waiter interrupts, placing them on the table between us before walking away again.

"I don't think that will work," he hedges.

"Why not?" I ask as I tip my head and ponder our predicament a little more.

"I'm seen on casual dates all the time," he explains. "I think we need to be more proactive. We need to appear more involved. More serious."

And there goes the final nail in my coffin.

"What did you have in mind?" I ask before taking a sip from my glass.

"I think you should move in with me," he says calmly, and I choke on my beer. He can't be serious.

"Excuse me?" I wipe at my mouth with a napkin. "I think I misheard you."

"No," he responds. "You heard me correctly. I think you should move in with me."

"You would be miserable," I promise. He couldn't possibly want to live with me. I'm messy and disorganized. I love to eat takeout and read in ratty old sweats from my alma mater. And my cats. Oh holy shit in a giant litter box—he has not idea I live with a ton of cats, and I won't give them up.

"I highly doubt that." He smirks. He looks at me with a ridiculous look on his face that can only mean he thinks I'm so cute while trying to get out of moving in with him. But I'm not ready to give up just yet, even though we both know he is going to walk away the victor here.

"Here are your appetizers," the waiter says as he places a bunch of dishes in front of us on the table. "And also some plates."

"Thank you," I say softly. "It looks lovely."

"Thank you," Jacob tells the waiter also.

"Okay, *I'm* going to be miserable." I change my previous statement as soon as he's gone. Chancellor begins to dish up several things and hands the full plate to me. It's actually a very sweet gesture from this alpha male. "Thank you," I tell him. I didn't expect him to serve me, to take care of me like this. I hope I never get used to it, because when he's finally bored with me and moves on, I will never be able to get over him.

"I'm not so sure about that." He fills up a plate for himself.

"Oh yeah?" I roll my eyes.

"Yes." He smiles. He's barely holding in his laughter at my frustration. "My brownstone is huge. We may never see each other," he promises.

God, I hope that's true. He might not find my little babies as wonderful as I do. I'm hoping he doesn't notice they're even there.

"Really?"

"Oh yeah." He grins. "My brownstone is one of the biggest on the block. There is plenty of room for all of your belongings and even room for you to have your own home office."

He trails off for a moment, and I can tell he is thinking very dirty thoughts about me in his home. I, on the other hand, am wondering how I can make him pay for using my own personal nightmare to maneuver me into this situation. And if he was paying any attention at all instead of getting lost down the rabbit hole of his own personal fantasies, Jake Chancellor would have seen the wicked gleam in my eyes that could only spell trouble. Oh yeah, I am definitely going to make him pay.

"Okay," I say after he's paid the tab and our plates have been cleared away.

"Okay?" he repeats like he's unsure of what I am saying.

Sure, I could fight more, but I'm lulling him into a false sense of security. I smile brightly at him like everything is going to be okay, when nothing is ever going to be all right again.

"Okay, I'll move in with you," I say, suddenly

sounding confident.

"You will?" he asks in a sudden show of doubt.

"Yes."

"Tomorrow then," he tells me as I stand from the booth and reach for my leather jacket.

"Tomorrow?" I gasp. "You can't be serious. I need time to pack and prepare."

"As serious as a heart attack" He takes the jacket from my frozen hands and holds it out for me to slip into.

"Fine," I snap a little. I've had enough for one evening. I need to go home and plot his tragic demise while I snuggle on the sofa with my pretty babies.

"I'll see you tomorrow at ten in the morning."

"I'll do my best," I say after clenching my jaw so tight I'm surprised I didn't hear my teeth crack.

"Good," he says before pushing me just a little bit more. "Oh, and one more thing."

"What's that?" I ask on another roll of my eyes. My mom always used to tell me that I was going to break something important if I didn't stop doing that so much. But still, I can't help myself when it comes to him.

"Just a little practice," he says cryptically.

"Practice?" I ask, clearly losing my hold on my patience. "What practice?"

"This," he replies, and then he hauls me into his

arms and crushes his mouth to mine. I had told myself I would avoid this, that I wouldn't let him break down my walls, but there is just something about Jacob Chancellor that makes me a little… *wild.*

He kisses me like a savage, his mouth plundering mine. And I know without a doubt I never stood a chance where he was concerned.

I melt into his body and my lips part under his. I just *let go.* He licks into my mouth and tastes like a sin waiting to happen. I moan into his mouth and take from him more and more. *I want it all.* Not just his body but everything. I want all of his laughter and secrets. I want to share his worries and fears. I want all of his tomorrows. Yet it's something I know I absolutely cannot have.

And for a stolen moment, here in a place hidden deep in the city, I think that maybe, just maybe, he might want that too. But that is the lie I would tell myself when I'm home alone late tonight and trying to force myself to believe I didn't just make the biggest mistake of my life.

That is, until one of his Secret Service agents whispers, "Senator, you have eyes on you." And it's like a bucket of cold water thrown over not only me but Jacob, and I curse myself for being all kinds of stupid, because this is exactly what I do not want or need in my life.

He pulls me tightly into him and holds me in his arms with my face tucked safely in the crook of his neck as he rubs his hands up and down my back. I let out a shuddering breath before standing up on my own, and I instantly miss his strength holding my weight up.

"I should go," I say softly, my voice filled with all kinds of regret. Regret for kissing him, for liking it. Regret for agreeing to live with him when I should have been strong and said no. Regret for not joining a convent the minute he landed back in New York, because one thing is clear. Jacob Chancellor is going to destroy me, and I'm helpless to stop it.

"Me too," he says, and I can't help but wish tomorrow comes slower than it will. I guess it's time to pay the piper, and his name is Jacob. "I'll see you tomorrow."

"Tomorrow," I repeat with a twinkle in my eye. I have to be strong. I have to make him end this ridiculous charade before I can get too comfortable in his home and his life, before he has a chance to break my heart. He smiles boldly in return, and I have no idea what's going through his head right now.

I guess I'll find out soon enough.

COULD
POPULAR
NEW YORK
ATTORNEY BE
THE ONE TO
STICK

SIX

Lady of the manor

No. Absolutely not.

"I'LL DO MY BEST," I replied as I pushed up from the booth.

"Good," Jacob said just as I was reaching for my bag. "Oh, and one more thing."

"What's that?" I rolled my eyes. I couldn't help it; he is so frustrating. I feel like the sexy senator with the dimples talked circles around me all night and I somehow managed to agree to everything he wanted. What the hell? It's like I'm stuck in his sexual pull. Every single time he flashes me those dimples I got stupid.

"Just a little practice," he said cryptically.

"Practice?" I snapped. I was losing my patience. I clearly needed to get out of that restaurant and soon.

"What practice?"

"This." And then he wrapped me up tight in his arms and crushed his mouth to mine.

I melted into him like Frosty the Snowman in July, and my lips opened under his. And when he licked into my mouth, I just lost it. I let out a moan worthy of a porn star, which is nothing like me. Usually, I am reserved and private no matter what, but with Jacob, it's like I become a completely different person. And I don't like it at all.

But that's a lie. My body burned hot and I pushed closer to Jake. I needed him. I needed him to touch me, to put the fire out so I could go back to my normal quiet self.

And all the while, as he held me in his arms, the promise of more whispered across my mind, but we both know that would be impossible, and even if it weren't impossible, it's certainly dangerous to my heart.

We were lost in the moment like a Shania Twain song, and then one of his Secret Service agents whispered, "Senator, you have eyes on you." And it's like a bucket of cold water was thrown on us.

How could I have been so stupid? Not once, but twice I let myself fall into a compromising situation with Jacob Chancellor, New York's most eligible bachelor. And I am grand prize idiot of the year.

I HAVE TO SHAKE my head like an Etch A Sketch to

clear the images that keep skipping through my brain, but after last night, I am helpless to stop them. Now, all I can think about is how I want a certain senator to kiss me. *Again.* Actually, I guess I should start calling him Jake like everyone else if I'm going to be his faux live-in lover. But a secret part of me deep down inside whispers I don't want to be like everyone else.

"And I like that you call me Jacob," he whispered when he thought I wasn't listening. I have to steel my heart against falling for his charm, because now I've talked to him and really heard what he had to say. Now that I've kissed him *and liked it,* I could really fall for Jacob Jefferson Chancellor, United States Senator and really get my heart broken if I'm not careful.

My doorbell dings, breaking me from my thoughts. It's Carter, my assistant. I called him early this morning and told him I needed help packing to move. He laughed out loud in his haughty way until he realized I'm not kidding. I, of course, had to find a way to explain to my second in command that I was moving in with the presidential candidate of the year. And I had to do it all without telling him the entire thing was a sham because I'm being blackmailed. Somehow, I sidestepped answering when he asked me about Chancellor's... umm... "credentials," and I was tight-lipped when he asked me about our whirlwind romance.

"This is not in my job description," he says when I open the door.

"But you love me, so you've come anyway," I say on a smile. I'm happy to have a friend with me for this move, even if I can't tell him why I'm moving. Carter knows I'm nervous, but he thinks it's just serious relationship jitters, not "I'm being blackmailed into pretending I'm in a serious relationship with a man running for President of the United States." Jesus H, that's a lot to take on.

"I do," he replies with a frown. "Although I'm not sure how much, since you held out on me. I thought you hated Senator Chancellor."

"You know what they say about love and war and politics?" I laugh. I'm trying to change the subject, but my efforts seem to fall flat. If I can avoid the truth, I'm not really lying, right?

"That the buttoned-up politician is a tiger in the bedroom?" Carter snarks, making me blush. "Because I need to know if the tabloids are true."

Of course he would ask that, and I can't freaking tell him the truth, because with all of my frustration over the pictures and Jacob and this stupid fake engagement to a man I want desperately but can never ever have is boiling up to the surface. I want to shout "How should I freaking know?" but I can't, because then he would know the truth is I barely know the man and couldn't possibly be marrying him.

"Carter—" I start, but he doesn't let me finish whatever it was I was going to say, which is probably great, because I had no idea how I was going to stop him.

"Please tell me he has a big penis, please tell me he has a big penis, please tell me he has a big penis…"

my less than noble assistant pleads while holding his hands in prayer pose in front of him.

"You are ridiculous." I roll my eyes. "Come in here and help me or I'll make you load Chevy into her crate."

"No, you will not, devil woman!" he practically shouts. "I want to keep all my fingers."

"Oh come on, you big baby," I say on an eye roll as I walk away from him and head back into my apartment. "She's not that bad."

"Not that bad? Not that bad?" he parrots, clearly working himself up. "She's not that bad? Last time we tried to give her flea medicine, she bit through my thumb!" I wince as he yells.

"Okay, that was… not great," I say, kind of agreeing with him. "But she was scared."

"She was scared. You know who was scared?" He scoffs. "Me! When she peed on me."

I let out a resigned sigh. There is no talking to Carter when he's like this. I can only agree with him and hope to move on.

"You're right," I agree. "She's terrible. Why don't you pack my shoes instead?"

"Yippee!" He claps and jumps up and down while he cheers, effectively spilling the beans that this was his plan the entire time.

"But no trying them on," I add, giving him my side-eye. "Your feet are wider than mine and you'll stretch them out."

"Boo! Hiss!" he shouts, sounding so much like one of my pouting felines in a snit. "You're no fun at all."

He's right, and I can't say no to him. He's like the baby brother I never had, so I agree to that too. "Oh fine. Try them all on. Have a blast."

"Yay!"

"Just pack what I need. I don't want to be hauling all my stuff over there," I say before I realize my mistake.

"You don't want all of your stuff there?" he asks. Suddenly, all of Carter's good mood is gone. He tips his head to the side as he studies me.

"I just mean, I need to take this all in baby steps," I try to explain. I force myself to look scared out of my gourd, which is not hard, considering I freaking am scared out of my gourd, just not for the reasons Carter thinks I am. "It's all happening so fast."

"It is, honey," he says to me and I watch the hardness of his handsome features melt into a tender expression. He's so fiercely protective of all those he loves. He's so beautiful inside and out it's not hard to see why his husband snapped him up so fast. "How are you doing with everything?"

"Okay, I think."

"No one would fault you if you didn't move in with him…" he trails off, and we both know that's not true. The press would eat Jake alive if I didn't move in. And if I don't scratch his back, he sure as hell won't scratch mine.

"I think we both know that's not true," I reply. "He's really not a bad man." I can't believe those words came out sounding almost normal. And if you buy that, Carter, I have some ocean-front property in Nevada for you…

He shoots me a you-must-have-taken-a-blow-to-the-head look. "He's not a bad guy? We've been avoiding any dealings with him for the last two years."

"I know that," I snap. "Maybe I was fighting my feelings for him."

Lord knows I was fighting something. It was my wayward lady bits who would happily hop in the sack for a night with Jake's trouser snake, but his cock clearly leads him down dark paths and would only lead to the complete and total obliteration of my heart when he eventually pulverizes it by being caught with some-one else in his bed—*as he always does.*

"I kind of always wondered."

He did?

"You did?" I ask him, because I don't even think I like Jacob, but love him? I don't know about that. Clearly, I have entered some gap in the space-time continuum.

"Yeah," Carter answers. "It's in the way he looks at you. You can just tell his feelings run deeper than surface level and always have."

Yeah, okay. I barely keep from rolling my eyes and saying those words out loud. They were bad enough in my head.

"Yeah," I whisper.

"Well, let's pack this bitch up!" Carter cheers playfully as he holds up a tape gun in his hand like he's an old west gunslinger, making me laugh. He always brightens my mood. He's one of those people who is just good to be around.

I fold a few more boxes to pack some of my favorite books, like *Rebecca* by Daphne du Maurier and *The Complete Works of the Brownings*. Things my mom always read to me. My grandmother's original copy of *Gone with the Wind*. And I top the box with my favorite throw blanket I love to sit wrapped up in while I read.

"Maybe you should go pack a suitcase or two of clothes you'll need over the next few days, and we'll stash those with the cat stuff until we can get a moving truck here," Carter suggests.

"That's a good idea. I'll go do that now," I say before turning to leave the room. I stop in my tracks and turn back to him, wrapping my arms around him tight.

"What's this for?"

"I just love you, okay?"

"Okay, honey," he says softly before releasing me.

"I really would be lost without you," I tell him before I turn to leave the living room again just as the doorbell rings. "Now who could that be?"

"Expecting anyone else?" he asks, suddenly on alert.

"No."

"Well the cat is out of the bag on you and the high-profile senator," he explains. "It wouldn't surprise me if someone was here to stick their nose where it doesn't belong."

I let out a sigh, already hating the direction my life has taken. "I can handle it."

"I'm sure you can," Carter says. "But just in case you can't, I'm here too."

As he pushes past me toward the front door, I see the muscles in his broad back flex and play under his white T-shirt. Carter is over six feet tall, and while he's as sweet as a teddy bear, he strikes a formidable pose.

"Well, all right then."

"Hello," he says as he pulls open the front door.

"I'm here for Ms. Sanders," someone says from behind the wall that is Carter.

"And who might you be?" he asks, sounding more than a little intimidating.

"My name is Logan, and I'm a staffer for Senator Chancellor," he explains. "I have urgent business with Ms. Sanders. May I please come inside?"

"If you're not who you say you are, I'm going to beat the shit out of you," Carter explains.

"I understand."

Carter seems to assess the situation before stepping to the side and letting a terrified-looking blond man who's all of about twenty years old. My guess is he's not even a staffer; he's a college intern. And if it turns out he's an intern for any news agency, reputable or otherwise, he's as good as dead.

The young man—Logan, he called himself—adjusts his tie as if it's strangling him. He's of a slim, swimmer's build and looks as if he borrowed his dad's suit. He's actually kind of adorable in a boy next door kind of a way. And he keeps eyeing me and Carter as if he's about to shit his pants.

"So, what do you do for Senator Chancellor's office?" I ask him with a gentle smile on my face. I guess I'm the good cop to Carter's bad cop today. That's a fun switch.

"Errands. I'm an intern," he explains.

"And where are you studying?"

"NYU," he answers.

"My alma mater."

"I know," he says with a sudden smile that lights up his whole face. "You're a legend in the Law Department there."

"Really?" Carter asks, warming to the idea of good gossip. "I always figured Clark Kent here was damn near perfect. Tell me she almost got expelled for partying or was the princess of the panty raids and everyone tried to break into her dorm room."

"Oh yes!" Logan rallies to his cause. "Did you know she staged sixty-seven protests her senior year alone?"

"Now, why doesn't that surprise me?" Carter drolls. "That was incredibly anti-climactic."

I clear my throat to stop this walk down memory lane. "And then Senator sent you to me because…?"

"Oh yes! I'm sorry," Logan rambles before holding out an unmarked package to me. It's just a manila envelope; there are stacks of them in every office in the country. It shouldn't scare me. But the last one I received changed my entire world, and not for the better. I shake my head to clear my thoughts before pushing a less than natural smile back onto my face and reaching for the envelope.

"Thank you."

"Senator Chancellor said to tell you that he had to work late and to make yourself at home. Here are your keys to the brownstone, and he said to tell you that he included the security code in a personal note inside," Logan happily explains while I grow increasingly angry, and my smile turns more and more brittle. It's becoming harder to hold on to. It wouldn't surprise me if steam was shooting out of my ears as we speak. After he insisted I move in with him—today—he won't even be there? "Here is my card as well, should you need anything else."

"Thank you," I say softly, taking the card from his

outstretched hand.

"I'll see that Ms. Sanders has everything else she might need for the day," Carter explains as he pulls his wallet from the back pocket of his jeans and slips one of his own business cards from it before handing it to Logan. "I'm the Executive Assistant to Ms. Sanders. Should you need anything from her in the future, please reach out to me beforehand."

"Of course," Logan says, looking more than a little starstruck. I think we might be in dangerous territory of poaching him from the senator, and I don't feel guilty about it at all. "Thank you."

Carter sees him out while I dump the contents of the large envelope onto the top of the kitchen table. My apartment is so small I'm really only a few feet away from them. I could hear every single word of their exchange if my ears weren't currently ringing. A set of keys hits the top of my battered, wooden table with a clang, and a handwritten note flutters down on top of them. I don't want to pick it up. I don't want to look at it. I know that when I do, it's only going to add to my mounting frustration. And yet, like the idiot I have become around Jacob Chancellor, that's exactly what I do.

I don't know what I expected to find when I picked up the heavy linen notecard stamped with his seal and New York office info at the top. I am willing to bet they have the exact same stationary in his office in D.C. as well. But it's the elegant yet masculine scroll across its surface that has me smoothing my thumb over the words that threaten to shove me over the cliff into a murderous rage.

Grace,

I have meetings all afternoon. Here are your set of keys to the brownstone. Your personal security code is 5652. Make sure to set the alarm for HOME when you are in residence and AWAY when you leave. Make yourself at home. And be ready for me tonight.

—Jake

In the immortal words of Cher from *Clueless*, "As if."

I cannot believe that asshole had the audacity to tell me to "be ready for him tonight." As if I am going to give him my body at the first available opportunity. And he's not even going to be there to help me settle in his palatial den of iniquity! It'll be a cold fucking day in hell before that asshole gets to win me as his prize. I'll die fighting before I give myself to someone so cold and callous.

Carter walks up beside me, completely unaware of my inner turmoil after he quietly closes and locks the front door behind Logan. He takes in the keys and the note.

"Bad-ass," he says. "Let's pack up the killer pussies and crash the senator's old money pad."

Carter's enthusiasm makes me laugh. "Anything for you, Carter."

"Maybe he has crazy expensive alcohol we can snatch and drink like delinquent teenagers while he's at work." He waggles his eyebrows at me.

"That sounds like an excellent idea."

"Great!" He claps his hands before he issues his orders to organize my chaos. "Change of plans. I'll pack your suitcases and you pack up the killer kitties."

"They aren't that bad!" I shout on a laugh.

"You're right. They are terrifying!" he yells over his shoulder before heading down the hall to my bedroom to pack up some clothes I will need over the next few days.

"THIS. PLACE. IS. *AWESOME*!" Carter's enthusiastic shouts can probably be heard from outer space.

Sometime after Logan left my apartment and I managed to not burst a brain aneurysm over Chancellor's callous treatment of me and this move, or whatever the hell it might be, Carter and I packed up my life as best as we could. He brilliantly labeled and ruthlessly organized in a way that would put high-ranking generals to shame. He packed my clothes for the next few days and my toiletries, and I packed the cats into their crates. It really wasn't as bad as it seemed. I did have to take a quick shower, because Panda got so mad he peed on me, but otherwise, everything went as planned.

"I think I'm going to have to order not one but two Uber XLs for these beasts," Carter said as he eyed my many pet carriers in the living room, each one full of a pleading cat. I just rolled my eyes and waited for the cars to arrive while I continued to pick up and organize. I also talked to my cats.

When the first car arrived, Carter, who I am now ninety percent sure was some great military general in a past life, had started ordering everyone around. I realize now his ultimate goal was to not have to ride in the car with the cats. And he succeeded.

One car was loaded with my two suitcases and several boxes of the cats' accoutrements—a scratching post, a kitty condo, food bowls, litter boxes, and more. The carriers were loaded into the back of another Suburban, and then Carter offered me a hand up into the backseat of the SUV. But as looks can be deceiving, my dutiful assistant was really just ensuring his own survival. He slammed the door closed behind me before I could even say one single word and then he ran—yes, ran—to the SUV behind the one I was in and hopped in.

There were a handful of photographers outside of Chancellor's New York home when we pulled up. Thankfully, I looked decent enough. My hair is pulled up in a messy bun and my makeup is soft and natural with a little pale-pink blush on my cheeks and a clear gloss on my lips. After my shower, I had tossed on a cute pair of jeggings and a fitted NYU crew neck sweatshirt. I took a deep breath and pushed it out before plastering a small smile on my face just before I pushed the car door open and stepped out into my new normal.

Flashes snapped around me, and I brushed a loose hair back from my forehead before turning to the driver to help him gather my babies to take them into their new home. I felt a pang of remorse; I probably should have warned Jake about the cats, but he wanted me to be the lady of the manor, and that's exactly what he's going to get.

"Grace! Grace!" they shouted at me. "How long have you been with the senator?"

I didn't answer; I just grabbed a cat carrier and the keys that felt like they were scorching my palm and walked up the concrete and brick steps of the senator's home.

"Does the senator know you have cats?"

I had set the carrier just inside the door of the vestibule before heading back down the stairs to grab two more. Carter was holding the press at bay while the drivers unloaded the cat boxes and my suitcases.

"Do you think he'll be able to stay faithful to you when every single woman in New York wants a piece of him?" one shouted, and I felt my composure slip just a bit before I smiled a brittle smile and waved to them as I walked up the stairs one last time.

I slipped my phone from my jeans pocket and sent off a quick text to the man of the hour.

ME: Thanks for the heads up on the press. That was fun.

JAKE: It's all part of the plan. Stay the course.

ME: I'm doubting the course.

JAKE: We'll work off that frustration and excess energy when I get home. You'll feel better after you come.

ME: Don't count on it.

JAKE: Be ready for me.

ME: …

I started to text him back, but really, it's not worth it. He will only keep arguing, and I wasn't sure his texting me about my orgasms was really beneficial in this situation.

"Jesus H. I need a drink after that," Carter said once he closed and locked the door behind us. "Let's go snoop around the senator's house and find his good liquor."

I couldn't help the laugh that slipped out. "Fine. Let's go." I mean, it's no less than Jacob deserves by orchestrating this whole thing.

"Would you get a look at this place?" he breathed as we started opening cat carriers and watching the angry little furballs flee the room.

I looked up at Carter to see him taking in the dark wood stairs and entryway, polished within an inch of its life. This home has to be on some historic registries.

"It's amazing what a lot of old money can buy."

"Your snobbery is showing," Carter said. "Besides, this is your home now."

"You're right," I told him. "Let's go drink his fancy wine."

"Solid plan."

After snooping through the palatial five-story brownstone, Carter and I didn't find anything remotely scandalous. I was kind of hoping we'd find some sort of den of iniquity, a red room of pain, but there was nothing out of the norm to be found.

We did find a fancy wine cellar full of expensive-looking bottles. Carter and I carefully selected two that looked expensive but not irreplaceable and carried our bounty upstairs. We drank both, laughing the whole time. And the whole time, I sat nervous, feeling totally on edge, but Jacob never showed. Which brings us to now.

When it grows late, Carter leaves for the comfort of his home and his hot husband. I can't blame him. I would be home wrapped up in a good-looking man who dotes on me too—if I had one. Instead, I sit fretting away the hours. What I should have done was scoped out a guest bedroom.

When I can't take it anymore, I pour myself another large glass of wine and climb the stairs. I draw myself a hot bath and try to unwind. When the thought of being caught naked and trapped in a pool of water makes me even more anxious, I climb out of the tub and dry off. I pull on a soft pair of black leggings and my favorite college sweatshirt.

I head back down to the kitchen, feeling the heat from the bath and the wine in my head. I need to add some food to my bloodstream to dilute the pinot noir. This kitchen is nothing like the small little galley number in my apartment across town. This is meant for commercial use. After surveying the contents of the fridge, I grill two chicken breasts in a pan and chop vegetables for a salad. I wouldn't usually be so nice to Jacob, but I'm going to try to sway him to my non-intimate way of thinking with good food and camaraderie. I'm going to kill him with kindness, and then maybe he won't ruin me for all other men and make me fall halfway in love with him.

Wishful thinking, right?

I pour myself another glass of wine and eat my dinner standing up at the kitchen counter. When I'm done, I clean up and place Jake's plate in the fridge for whenever he returns, which clearly isn't going to be anytime soon. The cats have started coming out of their hiding places one by one and are loving all the space to hide and run around.

I grab a book and my favorite throw blanket Carter thoughtfully packed for me and snuggle into a corner of a sofa in the den. Eventually, my fluffy Himalayan comes to cuddle in my lap. She always loves to snuggle when I read. And finally, I start to relax.

Ten minutes later, I'm totally spoiled, when I hear the front door open followed by the beeping of the alarm pad, which I forgot to reset when we came in. And all of this is followed by Jacob's quiet, "What the fuck?" and then a loud "Meow."

Looks like the surprise is up. I sit quietly on the sofa for longer than I should and am a little embarrassed to admit I consider hiding under my favorite blanket and pretending like I was never here at all. And in my still-a-little-wine-drunk state, I am completely honest with myself. My fear isn't that I don't want to sleep with him and he will force me; it's that I know I do. Even at his slightly angry words spoken in another room, I feel my nipples pebble under my sweatshirt. I want to feel his hand on my ass again and his rough groan against the side of my neck. How am I ever going to resist him?

"Grace?" I hear from down the hall.

"In here," I answer.

"What's this?" he asks when he appears in the

doorway holding a gray cat with one ear in his arms like a baby. And that cat is purring so loud he could probably be heard in New Mexico. Traitor.

"My cat," I answer blandly.

"And that one?" He nods toward my snuggle buddy, Winks.

"Also mine."

"So just the two then?" he asks mildly, and it has me more on edge than I was all night. Something about Jacob Chancellor tells me it's when he's quiet that I need to be more on guard than when he's yelling.

"No."

"How many?"

"Eight."

He looks to contemplate my answer for a minute before seeming to accept it, which makes me nervous. "Any dogs? Parrots? Or chinchillas?" he asks, and a little wine-drunk giggle slips out of my mouth. I bite my lip to hold it back, but it's no use, and an odd look crosses Jake's face.

But I don't think about it now. Later, I would realize I should have. Later, I would realize that I had let my guard slip and it would prove to be a fatal error. But right now, the sight of him holding my senior rescue cat like a baby has me all twisted up in knots and behaving like a girl with her first crush.

"No. Just the cats."

"Okay," he says, and he looks tired. More tired

than I realized before. Maybe his life isn't all sunshine and rainbows after all. "I take it you've had dinner?"

"I did," I tell him. "I left you a plate in the fridge."

"You made me dinner?" he asks in a voice that makes the hair on the back of my neck stand on end. There's something about his reaction I don't understand. He sets the cat in his arms down before issuing his next command. "Come here."

"I-I-I'm sorry," I whisper. Shit, I made him mad and I was just trying to be nice. How could I keep bungling this all so badly? "I won't do it again."

"I said come here," he growls. "Don't make me ask again."

I jump up and walk toward him, stopping a foot away from him. I know he wouldn't hurt me, but he still scares the crap out of me. There's something about him that just screams dangerous.

Jake reaches out and hooks me by my arm, swinging me into his body as he closes around me in a tight hug. He tucks his face into the crook of my neck and just holds me for a bit. I'm not really sure what to do with such a tender gesture, so I awkwardly pat him on the back, making him chuckle.

"No one's made me dinner in a long time, honey," he says softly when he pulls back to look at my face but still doesn't release me. "You didn't do anything wrong. You just made me happy."

"Oh," I reply uneasily. "Okay."

"Keep me company while I eat?" he asks sweetly, almost a little shyly, and I don't know what to make of this Jake. He's cute and he's funny and he's playful. I don't want to say no to him, but I also don't trust him to be real. But maybe this is how I sway him to my way of thinking.

Or maybe it's the beginning of my downfall. Only time will tell.

"Okay," I repeat.

He lets me go but takes my hand in his and leads me back into the kitchen. I let out an undignified shriek when he turns on me and scoops me up, unceremoniously dropping me on the prep island and laughing at my reaction.

"What did you make me?" he asks as he moves to the fridge. The way his face lights up, I wish it was something fancier. Maybe tomorrow I'll wow him with my mom's recipe for chicken parmigiana.

"Nothing special," I answer. "Just a salad with grilled chicken."

"Thank you," he says as he pulls the plate from the fridge and sets it on the island next to me.

"You're welcome."

He walks over to a bottle of wine Carter and I opened and examines the label. It paired nicely with the chicken, if I do say so myself. He pulls down another wine glass and empties the bottle into it before taking a sip. I get lost in the way his throat moves as he swallows the dry wine, and I'll be damned if that isn't more than a little tingle I feel between my thighs at the sight. He's so sexy I could probably come just from watching him.

He looks up at me, and my breath catches at the hungry look in his eyes. And I don't think it's from a boring salad and grilled chicken.

Jake prowls back toward me, and I have the sudden urge to run, but I know that can't be right either. It's like they say at the zoo—never run from a lion; a true predator thrives on the chase. And I know without a doubt Jake would too. Just like I also know he'd catch me if I ran.

I should run.

I take too long deciding, because he's standing before me and I haven't even moved. Shit. Jake takes another sip from his glass before holding it up to my lips. I open them just enough for him to pour a sip into my mouth. The move is so intimate, so raw.

"Going somewhere?" he asks, and it's like he knows. Jake always knows everything about me.

"Oh, ya know…." I hedge.

"I thought you were going to keep me company while I ate my dinner," he says as he sets the wine glass aside.

"I am," I say hesitantly as he nudges his hips between my thighs while my legs dangle off the countertop. "But your dinner is over there." I nod to his plate sitting off to the side. He doesn't even look toward it; no, Jake keeps his eyes firmly locked on mine.

"I think I found something I want even more."

And then he grips the back of my neck in his strong hand and crushes his mouth to mine in an earth-shattering kiss like I have never felt before. I feel his length, hard as steel, press against my center, and I gasp into his mouth. Jake does not hesitate, licking into mine. He tastes me and owns me all at once. My body is his to master, and I was foolish to think otherwise.

I arch into him, pressing my pussy against his erection. My entire body feels on fire. I'm engulfed in the flames he created, and I can't stop it. I rock my hips again and again against him as the pressure builds and builds.

He slides his hand under the hem of my sweatshirt and up, over the smooth skin of my belly and higher until his palm covers my unbound breast. He squeezes it as his hand flexes involuntarily. The minor pain only seems to drive me wilder, and I whimper into his mouth for more.

"Fuck," he bites out as he trails his mouth over my cheek and down to the side of my neck.

"More," I pant as he sucks my earlobe into his mouth, and he grinds his still-covered cock against my center, hitting my clit in a way that has me begging for release.

My movements become more frantic as I undulate against him. I'm so desperate. I need this climax that's barreling down on me like I need air. Jake sucks the skin on the side of my neck as he pinches my nipple between his thumb and index finger. Hard.

And I come.

Wave after wave rolls through me, and I barely register Jake sliding my sweatshirt up and over my head, exposing me to his view, and I don't even care. I feel the wet heat of his mouth as he draws my nipple deep into his mouth before letting it go with a pop.

He pulls my leggings down my thighs just enough to expose my bare pussy to his view. The heated way he stares at me makes me want to rip them to shreds and beg him to fill me.

"Fuck," he grits out when he covers my core with his palm. "I could feel how hot you are for me through your clothes."

"Yes," I pant as he slides two fingers into me and begins to pump them.

"Say you want me like I want you," he demands as he uses his other hand to free one of my legs from my pants and then the other as his fingers continues to drive me higher and higher.

"Yes. I want you!" I shout as he throws my leggings to the floor.

"Thank fuck," he bites out before crushing his mouth to mine as he holds me up by the back of my neck. I would fall to the countertop if it weren't for him holding me. "I need to feel you come around my fingers."

"Yes."

"And then against my mouth," he says, and he sounds like he needs it as much as I do, which by the way his thumb swipes against my clit over and over as he pumps his fingers into me again and again, is desperately.

"Yes."

"And then around my cock. Fuck you're so fucking wet. You're sopping with it, and I can't wait to lick it all up."

I can't even talk. I'm so close to the edge that words evade me. I need him so badly. And he knows it. Jake Chancellor seems to know every inch of my body better than I do myself. He sees me and knows exactly what I need to take me there, and he does so ruthlessly.

He growls when I tip my head back on my shoulders. I'm so lost to the sensations as he pumps his hand again and again.

This is it. I'm on the cusp of awesomeness. He reaches between us for his belt buckle. Yes! This is it. I need to be filled by him so badly. Our bodies are about to be one. I gasp as he presses down on my clit with his thumb.

Fuck, fuck, fuck. I'm about to come.

And then his phone rings.

"Fuck!" Jake barks, and it's not a happy in the moment one.

He lets go of his hold on the back of my neck, and I drop down to my elbows, hoping they hold me up. My breath saws in and out of my chest as his phone stops ringing and then starts up again. His fingers stop moving but he holds them tight inside of me as he uses his free hand to pull his cellphone out of his pants pocket.

"Chancellor," he answers and listens to whoever it is on the other end of the line while he stares at his hand on my body. "This better be good, Rick."

I feel my spine go straight and my body go cold at the mention of his political mercenary, Rick Donovan. Chief of Staff is too nice of a description to use for a viper like Rick, and everyone knows it.

"Yeah," he answers something that Rick asks. "I'll be right there."

I close my eyes tight as he pulls his fingers from my core. I refuse to look at him. I can't. And if he cared for me at all as a human being, he would understand that.

"Look at me, Grace," he says, his voice low and rough. I should have known better. Jacob Chancellor can't let me have anything. I'm just a plaything. "I have to go."

"I figured as much." I'm surprised my voice sounds as relatively normal as it does.

"This isn't finished," he adds. He eyes me ferociously as he forces his hard cock down the front of his slacks before rebuckling his belt. I don't trust myself to say anything, so I just nod once hoping that is enough for him. It's apparently not, because he grips my chin tight between his thumb and forefinger, which still smell like my arousal, and he kisses me hard.

And then he strolls from the room fully clothed like the king of his domain, which of course he is. And I am left exposed and cold and, as always, alone, an afterthought. If I needed a sign to set me back on the right course, this was it in neon glowing letters. This bucket of cold water thrown in my face was exactly what I needed to remind me that companionable distance is the only answer, because Jacob Chancellor will not ever care for me or consider my feelings. I am nothing to him but a piece of property, a toy to be discarded when he's done with me, or more than likely broken me.

So, I do the only thing I can; I pull myself up off the counter. I pick up my clothes from where he threw them around the room. I do not look at the prep island where he mastered my body like no one ever has before and without a doubt never will again. I just walk quietly up the stairs, where I take a quick shower and throw on a pair of pajamas. I walk down the hall counting doors until I find a furnished bedroom as far away from the master suite as possible and claim it as my own. I lock the door behind me and climb into bed.

And I did all of this without knowing that as he walked away from me without a backward glance, he did so with complete regret for having to leave me and climbed into a town car to drive him to his destination with his thoughts completely turned to me.

Instead, I cried myself to sleep, and my final thought before darkness finally claimed me was that I can't let this happen again.

A CERTAIN SENATOR
AND HIS LADY ARE
PLAYING HOUSE.

SEVEN

Pieces of me

Rain hits the window with a clatter. The light of the gray, gloomy day peeks through the curtains. It takes me a minute to realize where I am. Like somewhere along the way, I dreamed all this—Jacob, the blackmail photos, his proposition of a marriage of convenience, and then the way he used me and discarded me. Only now I realize this never-ending nightmare is my life.

I swipe my cell from the nightstand and look at the time. It's way earlier than I would usually get up. The cats aren't even bothering me, begging for breakfast yet. Guilt pools in my belly. When I locked Jacob out last night, I also locked out my babies after they were forced to move to a new home. I didn't think I could feel any lower than I had before, but it like seems I always am lately. I was wrong.

I toss the covers back and push up from the bed. I would stay in this room forever if I could—no, that's a lie. If I could, I would leave this house and never come back. But the paparazzi waiting and watching outside on the street made this already untenable situation even worse. Hopefully, it's so early that Jacob is still asleep in his bed. I don't want to see him this morning. I can't play it cool. I already showed my hand by hiding away in here instead of going to sleep in his bed like he demanded and showing him indifference. I've always been my own worst enemy.

I take a deep breath and open the bedroom door, cringing at how loud the hinges sound in the quiet hallway. I look both ways like a startled child crossing the road. I don't see him, but that doesn't mean the not-so-good senator isn't lying in wait somewhere, ready to throw my own failings in my face.

I scurry down the hallway to the bathroom and turn the taps to let the water heat up. I lean over the sink and get my face as close to the mirror as possible. If Quasimodo had a little sister, she would look just like I do right now. My face is red and blotchy, and my eyes are swollen and puffy. Seriously, if I saw me on the street right now, I'd think I needed and EpiPen and a bottle of Benadryl. To put it bluntly, I look like shit.

I strip out of my clothes and place them on the bathroom counter so I can gather them up later and put them in my hamper for Sunday Laundry Day. It's a thing. And it was my thing before the guys from *Jersey Shore* made it theirs.

I step into the shower in the guest bathroom and let the hot water pour down my body, letting my muscles loosen up one by one. I'm still not ready to see Chancellor yet so I don't go into the master bedroom where I put all of my things when I was busy pretending that the sexy senator loved me and his dimples and penis were for me alone. I pour shampoo into my hand and want to cry when I notice it smells decidedly feminine. Not that it wouldn't have been worse to smell that smell that can only be Jake Chancellor, but to know I'm using another woman's—*the real one's*—toiletries feels even worse. He might not belong to one woman, but Ashley Jeffries has made her mission to become his FLOTUS a public one. I've never been the other woman before, and I have to admit it doesn't make me feel all that great about myself.

I finish my shower quickly and shut the water off. I don't feel any better than I did before. Actually, I might feel worse. I dry off and wrap the towel around my body before I brush my teeth. I blow dry my hair with a big round brush so the ends flip in a soft curl and pin the sides back before carefully applying my makeup. I grab my clothes from the night before and sneak back down the hall.

Even though my world is probably ending any day now, it's still a workday, and I need to keep pretending until it all explodes in my face, and then I'll have to change my identity and move to Costa Rica. I was pretty decent at high school Spanish, so it's a legitimate plan. The cats and I can spend our days catching fresh fish.

But until then, I just have to keep on keepin' on.

I pull on a pair of lace panties and a matching bra before letting a black silk V-neck blouse drop down over my head. I step into a pleated silk skirt that hits at my knees and is covered in a pastel paisley pattern. I sit down on the bed and roll a pair of nude, lace-topped thigh-highs up my legs before letting my skirt drop back into place as I stand up and step into my black Louboutins. My diamond earrings and bracelet are currently accompanied by my silver Bulova watch my parents bought me for my college graduation, sitting on the dressing table in Jake's personal bedroom. So, I'm heading to work today for the first time ever without them. I just can't make myself go in there and claim them.

So instead, I make my way downstairs to the kitchen. I see the cat bowls where Carter and I stacked them yesterday. Was it only yesterday afternoon that I felt like, with a plan, I could see this mission through without losing pieces of myself along the way? How painfully naïve I was, but I know better now.

I lay them out on the counter like I always do and start cracking cans of cat food. By the time I'm done dishing it out, they're all lined up on the floor, watching me. I set the bowls on the floor two at a time, offering pets to each as I go.

When I'm done, I search the pantry for something I shouldn't want—sugary cereal—but Jake's cabinets are all full of things like Raisin Bran and Corn Flakes, and not even the frosted kind. I'm living with a monster. I pour some Corn Flakes into a bowl and then enough sugar on top to more than make up for the frosting. It's all part of my vow to gain forty pounds so no man will find me attractive any more. Men are nothing but trouble. My mom always said it was a lesson that could only be learned the hard way, and I like to think I just learned that lesson tenfold. I cover the whole thing with milk and give it a stir before carrying it to the small table in the corner of the kitchen.

I sit in a wooden chair and mindlessly spoon cereal into my mouth. I'm not hungry. I can never eat much when I'm upset, unless I'm *really* upset, and then I eat everything in sight. But this isn't one of those times. I need to fuel my body to get through the day. That's it. I just have to keep going. And then eventually I will find my way out of this mess. I hope.

"Don't do that again."

I should have been paying attention. If I was, maybe I would have heard Jake sneak up behind me, but I was too lost in my own misery to notice. So, when he barked his terse words at me, I nearly jumped out of me seat.

"Wh-what?" I ask. I shouldn't have, but I do anyway. One day, I'll learn to use my head around Jacob, but today isn't the day, and tomorrow probably isn't looking very good either.

"I said don't do that again," he growls as he boxes me in from behind.

"I don't know what you mean." I'm sure I do, but

I'm going to save face and gain some ground with him if it kills me, which it probably will.

"I told you that I wanted your ass in my bed every night, and I will not repeat myself. Having to drag myself all the way across town to clean up someone else's big fucking mess just as I'm about to finally get a taste of you did *not* make me happy," he explains.

"You weren't happy?" I'm so confused. I'm tired, and nothing is making sense this morning. To be honest, nothing has made sense for a while now.

"No," he answers. "And then when I finally make it home, you're locked away down the hall. But make no mistake that if you try that again, I'll take the door off the fucking hinges."

"You don't mean that." He can't. This is crazy talk. He acts like he wants me, but he can't. I don't understand.

"I do."

"But… why?" I ask as I look over my shoulder at him. It's the first time he's gotten a good look at my face this morning, and by the audible way he sucks in his breath, my dab hand at makeup hasn't covered up much and I still look terrible.

"Honey—" he starts.

"No," I whisper. "I need you to answer my question. Why do you want me?"

"I just do."

"But you could have anyone," I say, feeling my

frustration mount.

"I could," he agrees softly as he pulls my chair out and scoops me up into his arms before he takes my seat, planting me in his lap. "But I want you."

"I just don't understand," I say, and a look that I don't understand passes behind his eyes for a split second before it's gone again. I hate this. I hate who I become when I'm around him. This isn't me. I'm not some weak person—ever—and suddenly, after one night under his roof I'm feeling needy and insecure. I don't ever need anyone to reassure me of my self-worth because I know that I am a badass, but this woman is so far from badass it isn't even funny. I knew this was going to happen, I just didn't realize that the transformation would be overnight.

"What's there to understand?" he asks as he shrugs one shoulder. "You need me to clean up your scandal, and I want you. To me, it's a fair trade." Easy for him to say. He's not the one who's going to be left brokenhearted when he moves on to 1600 Pennsylvania Avenue and I'm back in my apartment in Queens with my cats. I know he thinks what he wants right now is a political marriage to me where we live a peaceful coexistence for the greater American good, but I know that this insecure person can't possibly keep his interest for long because I am already annoyed with her and she is me.

"Okay." I don't agree to anything, but I have to keep it together. I can't let him have more pieces of me so soon. I have to keep as many of them as possible so

I can be me. What happens when there's nothing left?

"Now let's talk."

"I have to go to work," I tell him as I try to push up from his lap, but he only tightens his arms around me.

"Grace," he warns.

"No, I really do have to go." And I do. I have a full docket today of cleaning up messes left behind by men just like Jake. Men who go about their lives as if the world is their playground and, with enough money, they can avoid any real consequences. I should hate them, but they put a roof over my head and those of my cats. It's also how I'm able to pull off projects like Open Arms for the good. It cleanses my soul after I'm done wading through the muck.

"Okay," he agrees way too easily. "I'll drive you."

There it is. I was wondering where this morning's other shoe was.

"That's really unnecessary," I tell him. "I'm in completely the wrong direction for you."

"I don't mind," he says, and then he smiles that wolf in sheep's clothing smile. Those twin deceptive dimples wink at me. They're selling me a bill of goods that will lead to nothing but heartache. And yet I can't turn him down. I mean, I could, but I would look like a big jerk.

"Great," I reply without any truth behind it, and we both know it. Jake's smile just brightens even more. "I'll get my bag."

SPOTS STILL DANCE IN front of my eyes as we sit in silence in the backseat of a black Suburban.

After I said I would grab my stuff and be ready to go, Jake called his driver to let them know we were ready to be picked up out front. He had met me in the entryway and held up my coat for me to slide my arms in. It was a sweet gesture, polite even, during a morning that was stilted at best.

It felt like there was a tentative truce between us, but after last night, it might have vanished into thin air.

I thought we would have a quiet ride to work in the early morning light. I was so very wrong. To be honest, after last night, there was not much more I could take before I hit my breaking point. The minute Jake opened the front door for me to exit before him, flash bulbs burst before my eyes. I felt stunned and a little scared. Only the day before, there were a few people lingering in front of his house, but today there were hundreds, and they were all shouting my name.

I looked back to Jake for help, but he just stepped up beside me with that politician's smile painted on his handsome face. Jake tucked my hand in his large one as he led me to the SUV all while wishing many of the photographers a good morning by name.

He was so poised and prepared it was almost as if he knew they would be there. I, obviously, did not. I was sure when I got to my office the internet would be abuzz with one terrible picture of me after another, while Jacob looks perfectly polished, a role I'm most comfortable in. But not today.

He opens the door for me like a true gentleman would for his lady and allows me to slide across the bench seat before he follows me inside. His Secret Service agent closes the door for us after Jake waves to his adoring public one more time. And then his agent climbs in the front seat next to the driver, and we were off.

But as we drive farther and farther away from the house and closer and closer to my place of business, I begin to wonder if I can keep up this charade forever. Jake slips the cloak of supreme politician on so effortlessly. And while I've made my career out of helping people out of messes and putting their best foot forward, this doesn't feel like a situation I can handle. I'm used to cleaning up the press mess from behind the scenes, not front and center.

"What are you thinking about?" he asks from beside me. I turn away from the window to face him. He's watching me carefully, his face strategically blank.

"I was thinking about what a fucking mess my life has become," I answer honestly. I feel like there is no room for prevarication between us while we live out this carefully crafted lie.

"Come on now," he says as the corner of his mouth tips up in the sexiest of smirks. God, I fucking hate him, and still my body warms for him and it's not even a full smile, just a smirk. "It can't be all that bad."

I let out a frustrated sigh. "It's basically a dumpster fire."

Jake throws his head back and lets out a real laugh. It rumbles up my spine and warms me from the inside out. I don't know that I've ever seen him look this way before. He's carefree and relaxed, not poised and in control. If I thought he was attractive before, that's nothing compared to how he looks right now.

"You're honest, if anything." His smile is genuine, and he looks at me as if I make his world feel right. But how can that be?

"I feel like with the situation we're in, there's no room for evasiveness between us," I repeat to him my earlier thoughts and immediately wish I hadn't, because the happy smile slides right off his face.

"I suppose you're right," he states, and a look I don't understand flashes across his face.

"I didn't mean to hurt your feelings," I murmur. "I'm in a bad mood, and that wasn't fair."

"I'm fine," Jake assures on a smile, but this time it doesn't quite reach his eyes.

"Jake—" I start, but I'm interrupted.

"We're almost to Ms. Sanders's office," the driver announces.

"Perfect timing," Jake says as he looks away from me and to the Tag Heuer watch on his wrist. I let out a soft sigh. What was I even going to say to him anyway? *"I'm sorry I accidentally hurt your feelings with the truth after you all but fucked me six ways from Sunday on the kitchen counter and then abandoned me without a backward glance"? Probably not.*

The SUV pulls up to the curb in front of the building that houses my office. The agent opens his door and steps down from the truck before opening my door for me.

"Thank you," I tell him as I take his hand and step down before he shuts the door behind me.

I begin to walk up the steps of the building before I realize Jake is just a step behind me. I don't even know how he got to me so quickly. He's like a big cat, prowling around without making a single noise.

"What are you doing?" I ask him.

"I'm walking my girlfriend to work."

"But you already gave me a lift here," I reply for lack of anything else. His walking me to my door is both romantic and terrifying. I need to separate what is and isn't real, and his being the perfect boyfriend is not helping me remember he is anything but.

"And I'll see you to your door," he says gently but with a firmness packed behind his words. He's not going to budge here.

"It's really unnecessary."

"It is," Jake says, his voice low in a way that says there would be no arguing with him about it.

"Oh all right." I sound like a petulant child, and there's really no helping it. It's exactly how I feel. I'd like to say I'm able to rise up from anything, but I would clearly be mistaken.

"Good girl," he murmurs from beside me as we climb the last of the steps and head for the elevator. I just roll my eyes.

I reach for the button for the twenty-first floor and stand back as we ride the elevator with a Secret Service agent standing in front of us.

"I've always wondered about people with an elevator kink," he says. "Until now. I can totally see the fascination standing here with you."

"We're not alone," I say, clearing my throat and nodding in the direction of his agent.

"Gus won't say anything."

"I'm sure Gus is a charming individual and exemplary at his job, but I'm not having sex in an elevator in front of him," I reply sharply, making both men chuckle. "And to be honest, this is the kind of idiotic bullshit behavior that will lose you the election if you're not careful."

"If you want to be technical," Jake says. "It would be behind him."

"I like her, sir," Gus says, never turning to look at us. He keeps his eyes on his post.

"Me too," Jake agrees.

"I stand corrected. You're both morons," I grumble while rolling my eyes.

"See?" Jake says to me. "I told you Gus was a good guy, even if he was a Marine and not a sailor."

"Oorah."

Men are so weird.

The doors to the elevator open on a ding. Gus is alert and ready for anything, including startling Carter, who is apparently here early, probably to get all the dirt he can. After Carter lets out an undignified squawk, he holds a hand to his chest.

"Jesus Christ. You scared me."

"It serves you right," I reply, giving him a knowing eye as I skirt around Gus and Jake.

"I have no idea what you're talking about," Carter says as he plays the part of the affronted.

"I think you do." The effect falls flat when he knows we both know he's full of it.

"Fine," he sighs. "You got me. What do you need this morning?"

"The Open Arms Project and the Conners file," I answer with a smile. "Thank you, Carter."

"On it, boss," He salutes before heading down the hall in the opposite direction from my office that sits at the other end.

I take a step toward my office, and I barely lift

my foot off of the ground before a strong hand wraps around my upper arm and pulls me back.

"Oh no you don't," Jacob growls from behind me, but after the culmination of last night and this morning, I am not in the mood for any more of his bullshit. I shoot him a blistering glare over my shoulder, but it's no use. He just proceeds to blister my ears. "Do not ever step around Gus again."

"But it was Carter," I try to explain.

"No," he says firmly. "Never again."

"But—"

"I said no," he practically growls. "It's his job to take a bullet for you, and you will let him do it if he needs to."

"No," I argue. "It's his job to take a bullet for *you*. Now, whether or not you deserve it is another matter."

"Yes, it's his job to take a bullet for me," he says. "And also for you."

I look from him to Gus. I want to argue that Jake is wrong and he has to let me live my life and do so the way I have always done, but he shakes his head, and it's a jerky side-to-side movement, letting me know I should abandon ship; all hope is lost.

"Fine." I push out a frustrated sigh. The last twenty-four hours does not bode well for my future if every time I have a say about something, Jake argues me out of it. With slumped shoulders and a defeated air around me, I slink off to my office. In all truth, I was hoping he'd decide I lost enough for the morning and we could retreat to our corners so we could come out swinging again tonight.

I was wrong.

I drop my bag on my desk and am just rounding the heavy piece of wood when I hear the door to my office snick closed and the lock turn over. The sounds boom in my quiet space like a shotgun blast, and I drop into my office chair.

"W-w-what are you doing?"

"I think you forgot something," Jacob says confidently, and for the life of me, I can't think of what I could've forgotten. There's something about him that makes me nervous, on edge, so it's entirely likely I did.

"What's that?"

"You forgot to give me a goodbye kiss. Now, what will everyone think if they saw?" he prompts, and I think, *Well that's easy enough to remedy.*

"But no one did see," I reply. "So it doesn't matter."

"Oh, but I think it does."

"Do you want a kiss?" I ask, and it sounds more breathless than I would have wanted, but he makes me so nervous… and turned on. I like his bossy side, yet I will never admit that out loud.

"I do," he answers, and I press my hands to the arms of my chair to stand up, but he waves a hand to stop me. "But not yet."

I tip my head to the side and study him. "I don't understand."

"I know," he replies low in his throat almost like a growl. "So I'm going to explain it to you."

"Okay."

"Last night, you did not sleep in my bed," he says as he ticks my transgressions off on his fingertips. "And then you locked the door to the room, so I couldn't get to you. Then you didn't wake up in my arms or with my mouth on your pussy, because of the previously mentioned. And then you stepped in front of Gus, which could have been incredibly dangerous—"

"But it wasn't," I interrupt.

"In another time, it could have been," he growls back, still counting that on a finger. "And then you did not kiss me goodbye. So now you have earned a punishment."

"Wh-what?" I stammer. "You can't be serious."

"Oh, but I am," Jacob purrs. "I want you to lean back in your chair and spread your pretty legs for me. You'll do that, won't you, baby?"

He's not really going to punish me, right? I thought that was a thing that only happened in books. And still, I'm hurt by the way that he walked away from me like he did last night. Can I really do this? Can I let him look his fill while I sit at the desk that makes me feel powerful? Am I powerful in this moment or does he hold all of the cards? And then I realize, maybe I can be powerful too. Maybe it doesn't have to be him or me. Maybe there's power in me letting him take. We're in a situation that can't be helped and, Jake is right, we could make the best of it. We could give in to this uncontrollable passion and let the wildfire burn or we could slowly hate each other when he seeks fulfillment in someone else.

So I make my decision to jump of the cliff with him. How bad could one little punishment be if we both get to come in the end?

"Yes," I whisper, because as much as I hate it, I don't want to stop it either, so my hold on the arm rests tightens as I lean back in my chair and spread my legs as wide as my skirt will allow. My whole body feels like it's on fire as my skin flushes with embarrassment and arousal.

"Good girl," he says as he slowly stalks a little bit closer to me. He stands just on the other side of my desk and watches me closely. "Lift that sexy skirt for me. Show me your panties."

My breath catches in my throat, and with a shaky hand I reach out and slide the pleated silk up my thighs, keeping my eyes locked on Jake's the entire time. He drops his palms to the top of my desk with a heavy thud, making me jump a little.

"That's my girl." Oh how I would want to be his girl, but we both know we're nothing but these stolen moments. He might make my body sing, but that goes for almost every other woman in New York. I'm nothing special, and we both know it. "Now push those little panties aside and show me your pussy."

I hook my fingertips around the gusset and pull it to the side, exposing to him exactly how much he affects me.

"Mmmm," he hums, and I swear I feel the sound between my legs. I barely hold back a whimper. "Tell me, are you wet for me?"

"Yes," I whisper, even though the proof is there right before his eyes.

"Touch yourself," he softly commands. "Show me how you make yourself come when no one is looking. Do you rub your pretty pink clit like I did last night?"

"Yes."

"Show. Me."

I touch my middle finger to my clit and practically cry out at the pressure. Sweet relief is within reach if only I take it—and Jake wants me to take it. I circle my fingers once, and then twice, reveling in the feel of my hand while Jake watches.

"That's it," he coos. "Faster. You like it faster, don't you?"

"Yes."

"I know, baby," he says, leaning farther over the desk toward me. "I know how you like it. I know what you need to take you there."

"Yes." Oh fuck, I'm so close. I'm going to make myself come sitting at my desk with my fake live-in lover watching from the other side, and there is nothing in this world I want more than to do exactly that.

"I bet you'd like it if I bent you over this desk, with your ass in the air and your pussy dripping for my cock. Wouldn't you?"

"Yes, yes."

"I would slide in nice and slow at first and let you adjust to my size, but only for a second."

"Mm-hm," I pant as I circle my fingers faster and faster, pressing harder and harder. Oh, God, I want this.

"And then I would pump into your tight pussy hard and fast. Over and over again."

"Oh, God," I moan. I close my eyes so I can see and feel his words. I want nothing else but for him to do exactly as he says. "Please."

"I would lean over you, cover you with my body, my chest pressed tight to your back while I ride you hard and fast," he growls low.

"Yes, yes, yes," I chant. "I'm going to come."

"I know, baby."

"Oh, God."

"Not God, honey," he says just as I'm about to tumble headfirst over the edge. "Jacob is the name you'll scream when you come."

And then he clamps his hand over mine, forcing the flat of my fingers against my clit, effectively stopping my detonation in its tracks at T-minus two seconds to go. I cry out at the loss just as his other hand grips my hair, tipping my head back as he crushes his mouth to mine and thrusts his tongue inside, owning me.

This is clearly my punishment. Maybe no one gets to come after all.

When he rips his mouth away at the exact moment he snatches my panties from my very body, he still leans in close. "Now, you'll have something to think on while you wait for me."

"What makes you think I won't finish myself off when you leave?" I snap.

"You won't." He smirks. "I'll know it if you do, and I'll punish you again. But if you ride out the want and be patient like a good girl, I'll make it worth it to you when I pick you up this evening."

And with that, he lowers my skirt to cover my lap before turning on his heels and walking out of my office, with my panties in his coat pocket and my dignity out the window.

HEARTS BREAK ALL OVER THE TRI-STATE AREA.

It looks like a certain politician is officially off the market.

EIGHT

Complicated

I must have sat in my chair for ages—it could have been minutes, hours; who knows? I only know I wasn't there for days in my mind, because Jake had left me with an ominous warning that he would definitely be back to collect me at the end of the workday. And as he still hadn't darkened my office door for a second time yet today, I can only guess that means it's still Monday.

Well, shit.

Eventually, Carter came to collect me. We had a pre-trial hearing at the courthouse this morning. He handed me the case file and briefed me in the cab on the way. Our client was going through a messy divorce and wanted his prenuptial agreement thrown out, because he'd gotten caught with his penis in a person who was not his wife.

I would never have taken a case like this. Men like this disgust me. They think the rules don't apply to them, and if they have enough money, they would be correct. The partners are clearly testing me and my loyalties. I met with their client and handled their pre-trial motions, and then I marched into the stuffy corner offices and reminded them that if they try to pass off bullshit cases like this scumbag's on me again, I will be out their doors faster than they can say "my bad" and hang my own shingle across town.

Granted, if I were to become First Lady, I would never touch cases like this again. And the partners won't know any different. To them and the rest of America, I very well may be the next FLOTUS and shouldn't risk my reputation or that of my U.S.-senator lover. Not that any of that has a lick of truth to it, but the partners don't know that.

I straighten my spine and shore up my courage. I am a brilliant attorney. I am living with a powerful and well-respected U.S. Senator—even if he drives me crazy one minute and makes me come with alarming dexterity the next. This law firm is lucky to have me. I repeat my mantra over and over again in my head, leaving out the part about achieved orgasms in record times, as I knock on the door to John Stanton's office.

"Come in!" he hollers. Stanton is the managing partner of the firm. The rest are as old as the Washington Monument and only have their names on the letter-head and their grandchildren in their old offices snorting coke and fucking the secretary pool. I like to stay away from the younger crowd as much as possible.

Damn, maybe it's time to hang my own shingle after all. I'm getting way too old for this shit.

"Can I talk to you for a minute?" I ask softly. I learned a long time ago I get farther with the men in this office acting demurely, and when that fails, I fuck their shit up. Legally, of course.

"Of course, Grace," he says affably. "Good to see you."

"Thank you." I make my way into his office.

"What can I do for you?"

"I just wanted to know who assigned me the Conners case?" I ask with more sugar in my tone than all the Kool-Aid factories combined. Apparently, I laid it on a little too thick, because I see Stanton's posture go rigid. *Good, you should be worried.*

"I'm not sure," he hedges. "Why are you asking?"

"Because I won't be working the case any longer," I say on a gentle smile.

"I'm sorry, Grace, but that just won't do," Stanton says, pushing enough steel into his tone that it left the "your job depends on it" unsaid. "There is not anyone else who could take the case. We're just that busy."

"I'm sorry to hear that," I tell him, letting my words hang in the air.

"I knew you would see reason," Stanton says with a smile for me like a proud papa. Too bad I'm about to ruin his day. "There really is no one who could achieve the outcome Connors wants like you can."

"This is true," I agree. "But I won't be representing him. That prenup is iron-clad. He should have thought about that before he paraded his mistress all over town."

"We don't let our personal feelings get in the way of doing our jobs at this firm," Stanton warns me.

"This is also true," I tell him. "And while I find the work ethic admirable, there are many things about Mr. Conners I find highly questionable and some unethical and very illegal."

"You're point is, counselor?" The tone of his voice is sharp like a knife and he is warning me to tread very lightly. But I would never defend someone like Conners and he knows it. Could this be the blackmail? Would my own bosses be threatening me so that I handle their dirty work for them? I've always known that they took on some clients that were criminals even if they've never been caught and tried. And I have always looked the other way while handling the legitimate side of business. Sure, I clean up their messes, but only those of the non-criminal variety. Could this be how they finally get me to take on the cases that I've always refused?

I'll have to think fast to get out of this mess. Maybe the senator's reputation is enough to land me in the clear even if only for enough time to regroup.

"It does not behoove the senator or his purposes for me to align myself, his fiancée," I say, pointing to my own person as I explain to him that I won't be doing his bidding on this case, "with certain persons. So, I'm going to have to pass on this case."

"I don't think Senior Senator Chancellor would feel the same way," Stanton says cryptically.

"I wouldn't know," I tell him, and when he tips his head to the side to study me, I realize my mistake. A woman would know her fiancé's parents, right? Shit. "We don't see each other often, and when we do, we do not discuss my job or my cases." Whew, that sounded reasonable.

"I see," he says. "Well, I will be sure to bring this up with him tomorrow afternoon at tee time."

Of course he will. Tattletale.

"Of course," I purr. "Now, I have to get back to my office. I trust the case will be passed on to good hands."

"Let's not be so hasty," Stanton says. "I'd like to check with the senior senator."

"You do that," I tell him on narrowed eyes. "I will be checking with the current senator."

"Of course," he says as he looks down his nose at me. We're at a stalemate. I can't see how my taking on a shady client would help Jake win the election. Could his own father be trying to sabotage him? I'm going to have to look into things and see where the truth really lies because someone is in this mess up to their eyeballs. I just hope it's not me.

And with that, I leave his office on shaky legs. Why

would he want me to keep such a shit client? Conners has money, but is it really worth it to keep him on? The fact that I'm going to have to broach the subject with Jake this evening does not inspire warm and fuzzy feelings in me. Not to mention the thought of tonight and Jake's lusty promises simultaneously makes my palms sweaty and my panties wet. My life is so complicated. How did this even happen in the first place? I've been so careful. I've lived my life in half measures all to build this life I wanted, and now it all hangs in the balance with chaos swirling all around me.

Somehow, I managed to make it down the hall and to my own office. I closed the door softly behind me, needing a moment to be alone in the quiet to sort my thoughts. Quiet. That's what I need. I slip into the chair behind my desk and focus on just breathing in and out.

I've almost calmed my heart back to a healthy range when my cellphone, sitting face-up on my desk, rings flashing my mom and dad's smiling faces as they stand in front of the Mendenhall Glacier in Alaska. I stare at it like it's a living, breathing thing as it flashes and buzzes around on my desk. I know I can't wait much longer. If it goes to voicemail, they will only get more desperate for my attention.

How could I have been so stupid? In the whirlwind mess that has become my life, I forget to mention to my parents that the cats and I were now living with a U.S. senator—fake relationship or otherwise?

I am in so much trouble.

"Hi, Mom," I answer with false cheer in my tone. I

hold my breath and hope to God they buy it.

"What the fuck is going on?" my dad thunders from the other end of the line. My dad was a brilliant attorney working for the county they still live in outside the city, ensuring that all children had access to vaccines and well-child exams. But before that, he was a Marine. He sounds like he's still ready to charge into battle at a moment's notice. I can count on one hand the number of times I had either worried him so badly or made him angry enough to speak in that way, with his emotions so close to the surface. Apparently, today I'm adding one more to the list.

"A lot." I laugh into the phone. "It's been a busy week."

"I'll say," my mom mutters somewhere in the background.

"How long have you known Senator Chancellor?" my dad asks, and his tone is still not a happy one.

"I've known Jake since he first came home," I answer. Fortunately, I never confided in my parents my complex feelings toward the man of the hour.

"And how long have you been involved with him?"

Shit. How do you make three days so plausible?

"It's been a whirlwind," I admit. "But it's been building for some time." There, that didn't sound like I've lost my damn mind, did it?

"Did you have to move in with him?" Dad asks, and I can't help but laugh. I'm thirty years old, and my dad still treats me like a fifteen-year-old virgin with her first boyfriend.

"Dad—" I start.

"I don't want to hear it!" he shouts.

"She's a grown woman, honey," I hear my mom whisper to him.

"I know," he says after he lets out an audible sigh. "We expect you both to be at dinner tomorrow night."

"Dad, Jake is a very busy man," I explain gently, while internally I am freaking the fuck out. This is not good. "He's running a presidential campaign. Who knows where he might be tomorrow night?"

"I know where he'll be," my dad says confidently.

"Oh yeah?" I ask. "Where's that?"

"Brooklyn." I shouldn't have asked. "See you both at six on the dot. Don't keep your mother waiting."

"Okay," I whisper.

"We love you," Dad says gruffly.

"I love you too."

"See you tomorrow." And then he ended the call.

I was wrong. My life could get more complicated. And all the while, I'm still wondering when the other shoe will drop with my mysterious blackmailer. I haven't heard anything from them since the original note was delivered to my office. I know real life isn't anything like the old *Magnum PI* episodes I watch late at night, but something still seems… off. I think back to the stilted meeting with my boss and wonder if maybe the perpetrator is closer to home than I thought.

I would find out much too late that I should have been paying better attention.

WILL LOVE LAST FOR THE ETERNAL PLAYBOY?

NINE

Better together

A knock sounds on the door of my office. I look at the small watch on my wrist and note it's much later than I thought it was. After the call with my parents, I dove headfirst into my caseload and my charity work, unwilling to let my mind wander back to what a clusterfuck my life just became.

Another knock raps more forcefully on the door, reminding me that I did not acknowledge the last one. It can only be one person; everyone else is gone for the day.

"Come in," I answer.

Jake pushes the door open with a frown on his face. He takes one look at me, and thunder rolls across his features. "Why aren't you ready to go?"

"I lost track of time," I answer. It's true too, but he

looks like he doesn't believe me. "I'll be ready in just a second. Let me grab my bag."

That seems to mollify him, because his posture relaxes just a fraction and he nods. I quickly shut down my computer and tap my files into a neat stack before slipping them into my large tote bag. I grab my phone off the top of my desk and drop it in my bag before tucking my chair under the old wooden desk before turning around to come face-to-face with Jake holding my coat out for me. I slide my arms in one by one and let him pull it around my shoulders.

"Thank you," I say to him, but he's not done. Not by a long shot.

He rests his chin on my shoulder while he reaches around me to button up the three big buttons. The intimacy of my back being pressed to his front while he's wrapped around me makes my knees weak and my breath catch.

With one hand pressed to my belly, the other glides up under my coat, under my skirt, and higher. I feel my body go rigid when I realize what he's doing. His hand grazes my bare ass and squeezes. Hard.

"Mmm," he hums. "My good girl."

"Yes," I whisper, and I'm both embarrassed and aroused. How could I let him turn me in knots like this? This woman isn't me, and I don't know how to proceed.

Jake slides his hand out from under my skirt and lets the material float back into place. His entire demeanor shows absolutely nothing. There is no sign he just had his hand up my skirt to see if I found a spare pair of panties to replace the ones he robbed me of this morning. His face is a mask of indifference as he holds a hand out to me. I reach out and take it like a lifeline and let him guide me from the room.

Gus is waiting for us in the hallway. "Good evening, ma'am."

"Good evening, Gus."

Together, the three of us ride the elevator to the ground floor, Jake and me in the back and Gus standing watch in front of us. It all seems so normal. Like he holds my hand in the elevator every night and would be more than happy to do so every night for the rest of his life. And I almost believe the lie when the elevator dings our arrival on the main floor. I wish I was paying more attention, not lost in the fog of "what if this was my actual life?" Because then I would have noticed the press camped out on the front steps of the building.

Lights flash before my eyes, and once again, I'm temporarily blinded. I'm stunned. I'm stuck, my feet cemented to the ground. And once again, Jake smiles his "I'm everybody's friend" smile and loads me into the waiting SUV. I don't take a solid breath until the door closes behind me.

How could I have possibly thought I could do this? That I could immerse myself in his world for any length of time? That I could put myself out there for mass public consumption day after day? I was so incredibly stupid.

And then out the corner of my eye I see him looking at me. How does he do it? I wonder if it ever bothers him to be owned body and soul by the American people. Or is this his true calling?

Regardless of the thoughts and questions bouncing around in my head like a pinball in a game machine, the ride back to his brownstone is a silent one. But this time when the car pulls up out front, I see the paparazzi waiting outside. I know what they want. I roll my shoulders back and clutch the handles of my tote bag tight in my hands.

Gus gets out of the front seat and prowls around. I know there are other protection officers around the property; I just can't see them, and they mean to keep it that way. Jake pushes the door open and steps out. He turns back to the car, where I am waiting for my turn to get out, and he holds a hand out to help me. I swear you can hear a collective swoon go up through the crowd. Jake Chancellor, knight in shining armor, U.S. Senator, and all around Prince Charming.

I take his offered hand and look up into his bright blue eyes with a teasing grin on my face. I carefully let my bag drop down in front of me to block anyone who might get a crotch shot. This engagement game is supposed to clean up our images, not set off a nuclear bomb a la Lindsay Lohan.

"Senator, over here!"

"Grace! Grace!"

Our names are shouted in every direction, and it's

beyond daunting, but I don't let it show that they're getting to me. I plaster a sweet smile on my face and give a little wave as Jake leads me up the stairs to the brownstone's front door. He looks back at me, and pride washes over his features. It surprises me that he's wearing his emotions for all to see. And also, it warms my heart just a little.

I smile sweetly to him. To anyone watching, we look like the perfect couple, so in love with each other. He looks at me with pride and adoration, and in my eyes shines a love for the ages. Too bad it's all fake.

Before I have a chance to react, Jake sweeps me into his arms and plants a passionate kiss on my lips in front of everyone. But while the move was no doubt calculated, the result could not have been. The second his mouth opens over mine, I clutch the lapels of his jacket in my hands and sink into him. The tether on his clothing is the only thing keeping me from falling right through the stairs into a big heaping puddle.

Before the kiss can really take off, Jake pulls back with a look of regret on his face and once again takes my hand as he opens the front door for me to enter. He follows behind me and Gus after him, shutting the door and keying in the code for the alarm.

"You did good," he says to me in a cool tone. When the silence surrounds us, I stiffen, realizing that the kiss, the smiles, all of it was for the press and none of it was actually for me. Again, stupid.

"Thanks," I say for lack of anything else. Harlow is padding down the stairs, and I scoop her up into my arms and bury my face in her fur. Her happy purring goes a long way to soothe my frayed nerves. I turn to make my way into the kitchen to find something to eat, kicking off my heels at the bottom of the stairs on my way.

"Grace," he starts.

"What?"

"I'd like to join you," he says quietly.

I shrug. "It's your house."

He lets out a sign born of nothing but frustration and follows on my heels into the kitchen. I set the cat down on the floor, and she scampers off to find one of her furry friends to play with.

"What do you feel like?" he asks me.

"I don't know," I answer before rolling my lip between my teeth.

"I can order Chinese or I can show you how awesome my scrambled egg skills really are," he says, and I can't help but laugh.

"I do love a good scrambled egg," I tell him hesitantly, and it looks like he finally relaxes. He smiles a bright smile when he answers me, and it rings real. He's happy.

"If you play your cards right, I might even add some cheese and roll it up in a tortilla." He laughs.

"Now you're speaking my language." Of all of the different versions of Jake Chancellor, this one puts me most at ease.

We chat a little, but not a lot while Jake scrambles a panful of eggs. He's as good at it as he claimed to be. I sit on a barstool while he pushes them around the pan one more time before finally scooping out a big chunk and artfully rolling it into a tortilla sprinkled with cheese. I carry our plates to the table, and Jake pulls a bottle of wine from the fridge and carries it to the table with two glasses.

Again, we sit casually in the kitchen and eat quietly. I know the time has come. I need to tell him about the Conners case and see if his dad really has reason for wanting me to take it. And also, tell him I have to go to dinner at my parents' house tomorrow night, and we can come up with an excuse for why he can't go.

"So… umm…" I start before clearing my throat and beginning again. "How was your day?"

Jake smiles at me. "It was all right."

"Oh… umm. Good." Shit. That wasn't exactly a stellar segue into an open dialogue. "Anything interesting happen today?"

"Nothing out of the ordinary," he answers.

I'm beginning to sweat. There's no way I can tell him about dinner or the fact that I have a sneaking suspicion his dad is trying to manipulate my life. I'd almost wonder if he was behind the mysterious package, but the idea is so laughable. Why would he blackmail me with his own son? That's crazy, right? But still. There is more here than meets the eye, but what is it?

"Is there something you want to tell me, Grace?"

Shit. I swallow the bite of eggs I had just shoveled in my mouth and it gets stuck on the way down. I gulp a big swig of wine to wash it down. I guess now or never.

"Uhh… yes, there is," I answer. We sit there, not eating for who knows how long, just staring at each other before I realize he's waiting on me to continue. "So, my parents called me today."

"That's nice," he says as he leans back in his chair with his wine glass hanging from his fingertips. Gone is the sort of shy, friendly man, and in his place is the predator.

"They… umm…"

"Yes?"

"They want us to come over for dinner tomorrow night. I'll come up with an excuse for you," I tell him quickly. "I already told them how busy you are."

"I'll clear my schedule."

"They'll understand. Don't worry. But I'll probably be home late."

"I said I'll clear my schedule."

"Oh. Really?" I can't help but ask. I wish I'd been able to hold my tongue, because he smiles a knowing grin that spreads across his face, turning me inside out.

"Yeah."

"Oh… well. Thank you."

"Anything else?" he asks, and the happiness in my chest slips away.

"Yeah," I say softly like I swallowed something bitter. What if this goes even deeper than I thought? Or worse, what if Jake doesn't believe me? Will our tentative truce be broken?

"What is it?" He looks suddenly alert. This Jake is all ears. Great.

"Today, I was handed a case that should be a simple divorce, but there's something about it that just doesn't feel right," I answer. "A lot of things aren't adding up."

"I'm sure you'll figure it all out," he says confidently like that solves the entire matter.

I let out a frustrated breath. "There's more to it than that."

"How so?"

"I never would have taken a client like this," I explain as best as I can without breaking attorney-client privilege. "He is immoral, unethical, and I'm pretty sure acting illegally in some ways."

"So walk away," he says as if I hadn't already tried that. I love when men think they can solve all of the world's problems with a single sentence. How nice it must be to feel like Lord and Master of their entire domain. If only it were that easy.

"I tried," I tell Jake. "But the managing partner of my firm made sure to let me know that not only is he unwilling to let me walk away from the case but also that your father wouldn't be happy if I did. And the more I think about it, the more it feels like something is wrong."

If I was paying closer attention and not lost in my own thoughts, I would have seen his body stiffen before he asks, "Who is the client?"

"Jesse Conners."

"Stay far fucking away from him and my father," Jake growls, and it startles me so much I almost jump right out of my seat.

"W-what?" I ask wondering where I missed the change in Jake's demeanor.

"It's a setup." He doesn't offer any other explanation. His word is final, and in his world, I'm sure it is. "Just stay far away from them and I'll take care of the rest."

"And about your dad?" I prompt. What the hell is going on here? A setup? A week or even three days ago, I would have said that that was ridiculous, but now that I'm being threatened with a stack of compromising photos, I can't help but wonder if anything is possible, or worse, if the two are connected to each other.

"He's a monster, and if you know what's good for you, you'll stay away from him," he says, his voice low and vibrating with anger. I feel a shiver snake up my spine. My grandmother would say that someone had just stepped on my grave and I've never felt like the saying was more true than right now.

"Oh, okay."

Jake scoops up our dishes and tosses them in the sink a little harder than necessary and I'm honestly surprised that they don't break before holding a hand out to me. "Let's go to bed."

Panic seeps into every corner of my body. I don't want to go to bed with this man when he's this angry. I'm not going to lie; he's scaring me more than a little bit right now. Maybe with some time, he'll cool down and then everything will be alright again. So, I make up any excuse I can to buy some time.

"I should really do those dishes," I tell him. "You go on up, and I'll be there in a little bit."

"Mrs. Summers will get them in the morning," he says as he ushers me toward the stairs.

"Who is Mrs. Summers?" I ask, when what I should be doing is running far and fast.

"The housekeeper," he answers. "She comes in the mornings after I'm at work."

"Okay." That actually makes a lot of sense. This place is super clean, and he doesn't seem to put a lot of effort into maintaining that.

My desperation to get the fuck out of here mounts as he pushes open the bedroom door, but I'm helpless to do anything but follow my Pied Piper into the room as he sings his less than merry tune. He leaves me standing in the middle of a massive bathroom with all of my face wash and lotions lined up on the sink. I take off my makeup and brush my teeth. By the time I'm done smoothing moisturizer onto my face, Jake prowls out of the closet wearing a pair of low-slung pajama pants. I'm a little taken aback by the image. I would have thought he was more of a sleep naked kind of guy.

I guess I was wrong.

"What?" he asks as he stalks closer, clutching a wad of black silk in his fist that he sets on the countertop before he begins peeling my clothes from my body. I'm so surprised by his gentle ministrations that I answer honestly.

"You have pants on."

"What?" He laughs as he unhooks my bra with nimble fingers.

"You're wearing pants," I repeat. "I figured you for a naked sleeper."

"I am," he says as he unzips the side of my skirt and lets the material float to the ground around my feet, leaving me wearing nothing at all. "But you seem to have had a kind of rough day, so I didn't want to add to that."

And there's the feeling of melting into a puddle of goo again. How can such a dangerous man be so sweet and thoughtful at times? I'm going to have to keep my guard up at all times.

Jake rolls up the material he carried in with him and lets it drop down over my head and around me. I slip my arms through the straps and marvel at the most beautiful black silk nightie I have ever seen. This didn't come with me, which can only mean one thing—our fake relationship just jumped to the lingerie stage. I wonder if Logan or Mrs. Summers procured this for me to wear to please him and it wasn't a nice thought so I try and shake it from my brain.

My breath saws in and out of my lungs and my heart thunders louder than the Clydesdales in a beer ad as Jake takes my hand and leads me to bed. He pulls the bedding back and I climb in. He follows behind me and then settles the blankets over us before turning out the light on his bedside table. The room is totally dark other than the city lights shining through the window.

This is it.

Jake is going to make his move like he warned me he would. I lie in bed and wait… and wait… and wait. And then finally, Jake rolls to his side so that he's facing me. He rolls me too, tucking me into his big spoon, my back to his front as he wraps his arms tight around me.

"Jake?" I ask.

"Yeah?"

"What are you doing?"

"Going to sleep," he answers.

"That's it?" I ask and immediately wish I could call the words back. I'm not ready to be intimate with him again after everything that's happened, and here I am, drawing attention the fact that he's not having sex with me right now. I have obviously lost my mind.

"That's it," he repeats, rolling farther into me so I'm on my back and he's got half my body pinned with his. "Did you want me to fuck you?"

"No!" I answer quickly, making Jake chuckle.

"I think the lady may protest too much," he says,

pressing his hard body further against mine..

"No, I'm good."

"You're not." I feel his eyes burning my face. Jake sees everything, and I'm helpless to hide anything from him. I don't know what to do with a man who is so attuned to me. "You've had a rough day, and as much as I want you—and I do want you, Grace—I'm not going to take you tonight."

"You're not?"

"No," he says. "So let's get some sleep."

"Thank you, Jake," I tell him sincerely as he settles us back on our sides with him wrapped around me from behind.

"We'll see how you feel in the morning."

And with that, I drifted off to sleep in Jake's strong arms, not once thinking about how it was odd I hadn't heard from the blackmailer again and really hoping that it's not my new fake boyfriend's dad because I could really like Jake if given half the chance.

COULD WEDDING BELLS BE RINGING SOON?

TEN

Meet the parents

"Is it hot in here?"

Jake turns only his head to look at me. The rest of his body stays facing forward toward the front door of a house in Queens. The house I grew up in. The house my parents still live in. The house we have come to for the inquisition—I mean, so my new fake boyfriend can meet my very real parents.

I'm not prepared for this.

Jake's face holds only a bland expression. I have no idea what's going on behind those baby blues of his, but Goddammit I wish he would give me something. I can't be the only one who is losing their shit here, right?

"No," he finally responds before raising his hand to knock on the door. The door which opens rather quickly after Jake knocked, almost as if my parents had been waiting on the other side of the door.

"My baby!" my mom shouts as she pulls me into a hug before turning to usher Jake into her home. She looks so happy—happy for me. Mom is overjoyed I have finally found my person, like Dad is for her. I can see it in her eyes. She's picking out china patterns and naming grandbabies after long-dead relatives, and that is not what this is.

Maybe Jake should have let that car hit me this morning. But I digress…

"GRACE! GRACE! OVER HERE!"

I had needed a bit of fresh air to get my head on straight again after another round with the partners of what their six-degrees-of-separation connection to the man of the hour could do for them. They were not impressed when the answer out of my mouth was absolutely nothing.

I get the feeling Jake is a man who everyone uses for their own purposes. He hasn't come right out and said so, but I get the impression his popularity is not all it's cracked up to be. And no matter what this thing between us is, I won't use him. I won't be like everyone else. Even if it costs me my job at this firm.

Every day since the announcement of our fake relationship, the partners have tried to slip me more than shady clients, assign me details to people I would never, ever associate with, and forge connections between them and their cronies and Jake. And I have thrown up every roadblock in my arsenal and flat out said "no" on more than one occasion.

And every single time, they've let me know that my position there hangs in the balance. They could be bluffing. It's abundantly clear they need me more than I need them. But they also might not be. I'm young— not that young but young enough that I'm not a partner. I also don't currently carry a surname that dates back to Kennedy connections, so I could be done. Fortunately for me, I've saved a nice little nest egg for my own startup.

Still, I needed to clear my thoughts.

If I had been thinking with a clear head, I never would have stepped outside the building on my own, midday like I did.

> Me: I'm going to grab a cup of coffee and I'll be right back.
>
> Carter: oooohhh! bring me back something good!
>
> Me: LOL. Ok!

He always makes me smile. I was looking down at my phone when I pushed through the front doors to the building. The camera flashes took me by surprise instantly and I stumbled. But I didn't want them to see me sweat as they called out my name. So I kept going, right across the street.

Too bad I didn't see the car that was barreling down on me.

"Grace!" someone shouted. I don't know who it was, I was too stunned. My feet encased in ridiculously high heels were cemented to the pavement. My heart thundered and there was a roaring in my ears so loud the horn honking was drowned out. This was it. I was going to die.

And then I was hit from behind by a linebacker, only he didn't knock me down. He grabbed me around the waist and hauled me out of the way just in time for the car to whoosh past with a honk as if it didn't almost mow me down.

"What the fuck were you thinking?" Jake roared, and it was so harsh, so mean, that tears welled in my eyes. I didn't do it on purpose. I just needed some fresh air and a walk around the corner to cool my temper. I looked up at him and opened my mouth to apologize, even though he didn't deserve it, when he took one look at me and hauled me into his arms, crushing his mouth down on mine. It was not a nice kiss; it was need and fear and frustration. It was punishing as it was praising. And I grabbed onto it with both hands.

"Get back," Gus ordered, and like a bucket of cold water poured over our heads, we broke apart. I tried to push out of Jake's arms, but he only held me tighter while the shutterbugs clicked all around me.

"Let me go," I whispered. I kept my eyes downcast. I wasn't ready to meet his steady gaze.

"Never," he whispered harshly. "Where were you going?"

"To get a cup of coffee," I answered. "There's a spot around the corner I like to go when I need to get away from the office every now and then."

"Then lead the way."

Jake held my hand while he walked around the corner with me to grab the coffee. I was shaking so badly I never bothered to ask what he was doing there midday.

"ARE YOU SURE IT'S not hot in here?" I ask again as I pull at the collar of my blouse. Jake just shakes his head once in the negative.

After mom and dad lead us into my childhood home, they sit us on the sofa to begin our interrogation. Jake seems totally unaffected, and my dad gives it his best effort.

"So what are your intentions with our daughter?" he asks as he sits across the coffee table from us.

"I plan to take care of your daughter, sir," Jake answers calmly.

"And you feel like you can do that by living with her?"

"Yes, sir."

"Before you marry her?" my dad adds.

"I intend to marry her," Jake answers proudly.

"Were you going to ask for my blessing or is that not something a senator does?" Dad asks.

"Dad—" I try to stop my dad from being out and out rude, but Jake answers him in the best way possible.

"I will when the time is right, Mr. Sanders. Being a senator does not make me above what is right and wrong," he says. "I will ask you when Grace and I are ready to take that next step, but know that with or without your blessing, I will make her mine."

I open my mouth to apologize to my dad for Jake's rude answer, but Dad just sits back and smiles. Something I do not understand about this exchange has pleased both my dad and Jake as they sit back and grin at each other. Boys are so weird. The moment causes a warm feeling to swirl through my chest, and I know without a doubt I'm in over my head.

"Dinner's ready," my mom shouts from the kitchen as she brings a pan of lasagna to the table. I rush to help her by carrying the salad bowl and a big basket of garlic bread. Jake meets me in the doorway to the kitchen and takes both from my hands, carrying them for me to the table before holding out a chair for me to sit in. Dad looks at me and winks before holding out a chair for my mom.

"How did you stay so calm during Dad's interrogation?" I ask Jake when I lean into him, whispering in his ear.

"SERE training," he says before winking at me. The answer is so ridiculous and lighthearted, the idea that torture and evasion training had prepared him to meet my mild mannered dad, that it catches me off guard, and I throw my head back and laugh, leaning into him while I do.

I was so caught up in the moment that I didn't see Jake's face soften and the look of complete adoration that passed across his strong features. Nor did I see the look my parents exchanged with each other when they saw how Jake looked at me. I did notice the rest of the evening went by with happy banter, wine, and food, but above all else, family.

**JEFFRIES'S INNER
CIRCLE CRY FOUL.**

ELEVEN

Meet the mercenary

"Happy?" Jake asks me as we ride in the car back to the brownstone. Dinner with my parents went so fantastically that I'm having trouble holding onto the reality of the situation.

"Yeah," I answer softly.

"Good," he says gently before hauling me into his lap.

I let out a little "eep!" before he settles me into his arms and tucks his face into the crook of my neck.

"W-w-what are you doing?" I ask. It feels like years since the office incident where he left me without orgasm and panties. And honestly, I had put the thought of it out of my head. I've had a lot on my mind. But now that he's holding me tight against his warm body, I can't help but be reminded.

"I'm holding you," he replies as he nips and kisses his way up the side of my neck. I tip my head back to give him better access, because I just can't seem to help myself where Jacob Chancellor is concerned.

"Okay," I whisper.

"And kissing you."

"Okay," I repeat just before he presses his mouth to mine. I open under him and let his tongue lick inside.

"And touching you."

"Uh huh." To be honest, he has been touching me in some way the entire time he's held me in his lap. Jake rubs his palms up my arms and down my sides, barely grazing my breasts. He trails fingertips up my outer thigh and back down while he kisses me over and over again, but the one thing he does not do is touch me where I need him most. I would think that maybe he's unaffected, but the hungry way he kisses me proves otherwise. As does the hard length that presses against my ass through our clothes.

I'm so desperate for him that I'm about to open my mouth and beg him to take me in this town car, when he pulls back and smiles sweetly at me.

"We're home."

"Oh."

Jake pushes open the door and holds his hand out for me. I take it without question and let him lead me into the dark house. I'm also going to let him lead me upstairs and put us both out of our misery. Maybe after a couple shared orgasms we will be able to put things back into perspective, and I won't hold out hope for when he will ask my dad for his blessing—something we both know will never happen—even though the more time I spend with Jake, the more I could let myself hope for it to happen. I know what Ashley Jeffries must have felt before she was given her final goodbye.

He keys off the alarm and shuts the door behind us.

"Where were we?" he asks with a sexy smirk playing about his lips when he turns back to me.

"We were about to talk about the events that need to be added to the schedule," someone says from behind Jake, making us both go solid.

I peer over his shoulder and see a man I knew I was going to have to engage at some point in time, and yet I was foolishly hoping that day would never come. Standing in the doorway to the kitchen is none other than Rick Donovan, Jake's Campaign Manager and all-around political mercenary.

Jake lets out a heavy sigh and hangs his head, because he knows that whatever brought Rick here tonight can't be great and also stopped the mutual orgasms we were hoping for in their tracks. While I find Rick to be completely distasteful and would never associate with him regularly, I can't help but be thankful for the distraction. Maybe I'll be able to clear the fog of lust and longing for things I can't have. Then I can go to bed with my panties still on my person and my heart still belonging to me.

Wishful thinking, right?

"I'll just leave you two to it," I say softly as I nod in the direction of the stairs.

"This involves you too," Rick inserts before turning on his heels and stalking back into the kitchen. I can't help but prickle at the way he orders me around without outright doing so. I'm not his political lackey. I stomp into the kitchen behind him with Jake's chuckle floating behind me as he follows.

"Excuse you," I snap. "I am not yours to order around."

"Are you dating Jake?" he asks me.

I want to deny it, but I also don't know who Jake has told and who he hasn't about the nature of our situation. Not to mention he had me so turned on in the car with barely a kiss and a touch that I would be lying if I said otherwise.

"Yes," I bite out.

"And are you living in his home?" This is really annoying.

"Rick—" Jake starts, but I don't let him wiggle me off of Rick's hook. Jake should see the kind of man he keeps company with.

"Yes."

"Then his obligations become your obligations," Rick says before pressing on and telling me something I already know and should have remembered, making guilt flood my system. "His obligations could mean the win or the loss of a presidential election."

"You're right," I reply quietly. And he is. I won't let my petty childishness cost Jake his election. Jake is somehow friends with this henchman, so I guess I should hear him out. "What do you need?"

"A charity gala," he says, and Jake groans, making Rick shoot him a glare. "You need to go out with Grace as a couple. It will go a long way to show you are more stable—a family man. That you can handle the running of the most powerful nation."

"I can handle it," Jake growls.

"I know that," Rick says, rolling his eyes. "But we have to get to the Oval first before you can show everyone else. Not to mention it will be a great opportunity for Grace to rub elbows for her Open Arms project. Thanks for including us on that, by the way," he adds sarcastically.

"Umm… I'm sorry?" I wince. I feel bad now that we all know that I left them out of it on purpose and the fact that Rick just tossed that less than stellar action of mine on the table like a dead fish.

"Consider us included," Rick answers, and Jake smiles broadly. Those two must have planned this all along. How sneaky of them! And still, I smile right along with them. Jake's joy over his boon is hard to ignore.

"Don't think we won't talk about that later," he whispers in my ear.

"Pay attention, kids." Rick claps his hands like and

angry school marm.

"Yes, Mom." Jake laughs. "What else?"

"In two weeks, everyone will need to be in Ohio to campaign."

I never really thought I would be part of Jake's campaign. How will parading me around as his serious girlfriend look when, after he's elected, I go back to my old life. Things are still too new for me to believe that Jake will want me to tag along all the way to D.C. with him.

"Grace as well," Jake says.

"Obviously," Rick responds.

"Is that really a good idea?" I ask, and both men turn to look at me. "I just mean that it's really soon. What if we don't work out? How will that look then?"

"Ahh, young love," Rick says sarcastically. "I don't care if it truly ends in a month, a year, or two. I care what looks good. So to the public eye, be the happy bride, figure out your FLOTUS platform, pop out some pretty political babies, and in eight years, do whatever the fuck you want. Until then, you're mine."

I take back every nice-ish thing I just thought about Rick. He's a douche. I see that clearly now. Unfortunately, he's also right. I need them more than they need me. Whether he knows it or not. I'm in this up to my eyeballs, and there is no turning back now.

"So what's the weather like in Ohio?" I ask.

"Cold," Rick replies.

"Anything else I need to know?"

"Dress classically stylish. I can arrange for some-one to dress you," he says eyeing me up and down like a prized bull at auction. "But looking at you, I don't think you need it."

"Thank you," I say reluctantly because while his statement is really disgusting, it's also true because I'm the shit and my stylist is even better. I'd be lost without Cara. But I don't mention that now, I'll have Carter add her to the team itinerary later.

"Do you need a hair and makeup person?" he asks.

"No. I have one," I answer. "I'll call her tomorrow. She'll have to have time to arrange for her daughter to stay with her grandma, so I'll need firm dates before you go."

"On it."

"What just happened here?" Jake asks.

"Your girl and I are taking over the world. Uniting for a common goal," Rick tells him without missing a beat.

"God, help us all," Jake says seriously.

"Hey!" I laugh.

"Did you know that there is a one-eyed cat staring at me," Rick says.

"Be nice to Winks, douche," Jake laughs before scooping up my cat and holding him like a newborn baby.

"You have a cat now?" he asks. "A dog I could

have used. But this will still work."

"I have eight now," Jake says rolling his eyes. I wonder if he's used to Rick's political machinations by now.

"Eight?" Rick laughs with a smile that finally meets his eyes like he's truly happy for his friend. "I never thought I'd see the day."

"Eight," Jake confirms with another answering chuckle and a shake of his head from Rick.

"Veteran's Gala tomorrow night. Ball gown. Tux. Make pretty eyes at him while grabbing votes. Lather, rinse, repeat," Rick says on a laugh as he pushes up from the table. "I'll attend the gala with you, so I'll pick you two up here with the car."

"Sounds good, brother." Jake grips him in a man hug.

"See you later," Rick responds. "Don't do anything I wouldn't do."

"Get out of here, Monk. I don't need that kind of negativity in my life."

Rick just laughs before he shows himself out.

"Now, where were we?" Jake asks, turning to me after setting the cat back on the floor where he scampers off.

I feel like a deer caught in headlights. "Uhh…"

"That's what I thought too," he says just before his mouth descends on mine. I could have stopped him. I had plenty of time. But did I? Absolutely not. I am firmly caught in Jake Chancellor's web. "Let's go to bed, Grace."

I whimper when he pulls away from me. I miss the heat of his body pressed against mine instantly. I think that's it. He's going to make me follow him up the stairs like a sad little puppy, and oh how I would go willingly for the spectacular orgasms he is promising me. And also, how sad does that make me? But it is what it is. When he scoops me up in his arms like a bride, I let out a squeal of surprise. My startled reaction makes Jake chuckle low in his throat, and I swear I feel the vibration between my legs.

I tuck myself into his arms as he makes his way up the stairs, never once showing any kind of strain from carrying my person around. Instead, he makes me feel precious and light as a feather. I am a powerhouse in this town. I am someone to be respected and sometimes feared, but to be revered and cherished is new for me, and I'm not going to lie; the heady feeling could easily become addictive.

Jake stalks into the master bedroom like a hungry lion. He kicks the door closed without a backward glance and continues to move through the room like a man on a mission. He stops just before the bed and slowly lowers my feet to the ground while holding me close. I feel every contour of muscle under his clothes and his hard cock as I slide down the front of his body.

"Jake," I whisper. I'm not entirely sure what I'm asking for. For him to slow down or speed things up. I don't know. I only know what I *need*.

He pulls my silk blouse free from my slacks and slowly, ever so slowly, gathers the material in his hands as he bunches it up and pulls it over my head before dropping it to the carpet. Next, Jake glides his calloused hands up my ribcage before reaching behind me and unhooking my bra with nimble fingers. I whimper as the cool air hits my heated skin. Gently, Jake brushes the tip of one nipple with the back of his hand, making me gasp.

"You're so fucking beautiful," he says as he watches the tip darken under his touch. I don't know what to say to that, so I just stay silent. I can't let him think his words affect me as much as they do.

My body jerks a bit as he grabs the buckle of the slim belt that circles my hips and undoes it. Jake yanks the thin strip of patent leather free from the loops of my slacks and tosses it to the floor with the rest of my clothes.

With stuttered movements, he reaches for the tie around his neck and pulls the knot loose before slipping the paisley silk over his head. He reaches for his cufflinks, his suit coat discarded somewhere downstairs along with my heels, but I stop him, reaching for his wrist. I hold him in my soft hands and pop the gold link free, first one and then the other. I look up at his face and see an emotion I can't name burn so bright across his sharp features that it takes my breath away. I hold my palm up with the cufflinks in it and he plucks them from my upturned hand before shoving them in his pants pocket.

I reach for the buckle of his belt and he grabs my wrist in his hand, stopping me. "If you touch me now, honey, it'll be over too soon."

I stand as still as I can while Jake undoes the front of my slacks and pushes them to the floor. I step out of them and kick them aside, leaving me in nothing but a lace thong.

"Get on the bed," Jake orders, and I turn away from him and climb up the foot of the bed, but when I get on my hands and knees, he stops me with a firm hand on my hip.

"Jake?" I can't help but wonder if I've done something wrong.

He doesn't say anything in response. Instead, he peels my thong down my thighs to just above my knees. He slips it past one knee and then the other before spreading my legs just enough to open me to his gaze. I feel exposed, raw. I'm open for him to view and judge. I want to cover myself. I want to run and hide. And I'm just getting the courage to do so when he rasps his tongue up the length of my slit.

His hands burn hot brands on the cheeks of my ass, pulling me apart. I clench the covers in my hands as he parts my seam with his thumbs and spears my pussy with his tongue.

"Oh, God," I moan and bury my face in the duvet. His tongue pierces me over and over as he holds me tight in his hands. Jake holds me just where he wants so he can consume me. It's raw and carnal, and I love every single moment of it.

He moves farther down and sucks my clit into his mouth. I writhe against the bedding, the rough brocade material abrading my sensitive nipples as I try to pull away or get closer—I don't know which.

"Jake," I plead, my voice high and needy, but he doesn't let up. I need…. Oh, God, I need so much. I can't even articulate the how or the why. Fortunately, I don't have to, because Jake sucks harder, rolling his tongue along my clit, and I splinter apart.

My breath saws in and out of my chest, and I sprawl out on top of the bed. I would move if I could, but I can't, so I don't even try. I don't even care.

I hear the slide of his zipper rasp in the quiet room and his clothes hit the floor before I am scooped up in his strong arms, and the heat from his hard body warms me all over again. Gently, Jake places me on my back with my head on the pillows. He looms over me with a tender look on his handsome face. He brushes my hair back as a smirk plays on his lips.

"Poor baby," he says softly. "I've been too rough with you."

"I'm okay." It was raw and it was intense, but it was also life altering. I don't want Jake to think I'm not okay, when I most definitely am.

"I'll make it better," he promises as he covers me with his body.

"Oh… okay," I whisper just before his head slowly descends and his lips sear mine. I open underneath him and let his tongue sweep into my mouth.

He slides the tip of his cock against my center, and he is equal parts exactly where I want him and not at all.

Jake trails his mouth across my cheek and down the side of my neck as he rocks against me. I open my legs wider in an effort to move him where I want him, and he just smiles against the side of my neck. The slow-burn pace Jake is setting is only driving me more and more crazy by the minute.

Just when I think I'll die if he doesn't take me, Jake takes each of my hands in one of his and intertwines our fingers together on either side of my head just before I feel the very tip of him where I need him most. And then in one torturously slow movement, he slides in deep.

I let out a gasp at the feeling of him filling me up. He's stretching me from the inside out and there is a tiny twinge of pain because he is so big. I hold my breath and wait for it to pass. So does Jake, because he holds perfectly still with my hands clutched in either of his and his forehead resting on mine as he fills me. He surrounds me with himself, and I am lost in the feel of him.

And then he starts to move.

"Jake," I whisper.

Slowly, he slides almost all the way out of me and then pushes back in again and again. The slide of him hits something inside me, lighting me up while he tips his hips down and grinds his pelvis against my clit. I feel like a box of matches that someone's thrown in a fire. Sparks light my skin, and I arch against him. His nose brushes the side of mine, and I breathe in his exhalations.

The way he holds me tight has me spread open for him to use for his pleasure but also to give me my own, and I love the feel of it. I love the way he commands my body to heights I never knew were possible.

I whimper as he moves faster, but his pace is still maddeningly slow. This isn't the hard fuck I thought Jake Chancellor would give me then be done with me; this is so much more. Jake presses his mouth to mine and his tongue presses between my lips as he grinds against my clit again, and I'm so close. I can almost come. I need it so badly, but still, he doesn't give me what I want.

"Jake, Jake, Jake, Jake…" I plead as I say his name over and over again like a benediction, but instead of putting me out of my misery, Jake slows his pace and pulls back, making his thrusts shallow. He doesn't hit any of my buttons this way, and I want to cry.

"Not yet, princess." Sweat drips down his toned body and adds another layer of sensation to my already overstimulated system.

"Please!" I cry out as I wrap my legs around his waist and try to muscle him deeper, but he just chuckles. "Please. I need you."

"Music to my ears, sweetheart," he says before giving me more of his weight as he thrusts deep inside me.

"Yes," I hiss. Oh yes, this is exactly what I need.

Jake presses his mouth to mine as he pumps faster and faster. Oh, God, yes, I need him faster still. Harder too. He seems to know exactly what I need, because he gives me both. I arch my back to meet him thrust for thrust as Jake takes me higher and higher, and I hold onto him for dear life.

He growls into my mouth as he drives harder, and then my world seems to fracture and fly apart. I am only grounded where he holds my hands tight in his and where he pumps his cock into my center over and over again.

And just when I think I might die, it's too much, the feel of him in me, around me, is more than I can bare, Jake throws his head back as he plants his cock deep inside me and roars out his release. I watch his beautiful face as he grits his teeth and closes his eyes. Watching Jacob Chancellor come is the single most erotic thing I have ever experienced.

He presses soft, open-mouth kisses all over my face as he gently glides in and out of my center before he slips free, and then he wraps me tight in his arms and rolls to his back so I'm sprawled over his large body.

Jake gently trails his fingertips over my spine, up and down and all over. After a while, his gentle touches turn a little more heated. I lean forward to kiss and touch him as well. He seems to become a little more wild as I take my turn over and over. And when I sit up to trace the indentations of his abs, he follows me up so he's sitting and I'm straddling his lap.

Jake leans forward and sucks my nipple into his mouth gently, rolling his tongue over the tip and making me whimper. I grip his hair in my fingers and arch into him, desperate for more. As I become more restless on his lap, I feel his hard cock against my backside and rise up to take him inside me as I wrap my legs around his waist.

We rock our hips together as we kiss and touch and taste each other, and in the end, we find release together in each other's arms.

Jake holds me for a moment as our heartbeats slow together, and then he rolls me back to the bed and slips free from my body. After what we've just shared, I hate the loss of him. He tucks my back to his front and pulls the covers over us. And I fall asleep in his arms, never once thinking about blackmail.

LOOKS LIKE
OUR FAVORITE
IT COUPLE
CAN'T GET
ENOUGH OF
EACH OTHER.

TWELVE

"**Y**es!" I gasp as I come awake, my body overheated and dangerously close to the climax Jake has obviously been working me toward while I was still asleep.

He holds me tight in his arms, his body wrapped around mine while his fingers move hard and fast over my clit. I let my head drop back to rest on his chest, and I grab onto his forearm where it winds down my belly, his hand playing between my legs. I dig my nails into his skin. I feel like I'm about to come out of my skin, this orgasm building hotter and faster, and I'm not sure I will be able to take it.

"That's it; that's my girl," he coos.

"Jake," I whisper, my voice harsh to my own ears, but I can't help it. I'm being consumed by the flames that lick up my body. "I can't."

"You can."

He pumps his fingers into my waiting pussy and curves them inside as his thumb presses down on my clit. I shake my head back and forth, because it's too much; it's too big. I feel like a balloon on a tether, threatening to be swept away by the wind.

"Oh, God," I whimper as Jake moves his fingertips back to circle my clit again and again, faster and faster.

"That's it," he growls, and he moves his hand faster still. His other arm holds me tight against him.

"Jake, Jake, Jake," I plead just before I burst into a million tiny, sparkly pieces.

The beating of my heart is whooshing in my ears and sweat slicks my skin. My breath rasps out of my lungs as Jake rolls me over to my belly. He arranges my knees underneath me and spreads them apart. I'm glad he has the wherewithal to do so, because I'm pretty sure I'm dead.

And then he grips my hips in his strong hands and drives in deep.

Somewhere along the way, Jake lost the last shred of his control. I grip the sheets in my hands and hold on tight as he plunges in over and over again. He sets a punishing rhythm I am already lost to.

"Fuck!" he growls. "Fuck, I need you so bad."

"You have me," I promise. I don't know where that comes from, and I know I shouldn't promise anything else to Jacob Chancellor, but I can't help it. I'm helpless where he's concerned. And if I were honest with myself, I would admit he owns me, body and soul.

"Just like this," he grits out as he grabs my hair in his fist and pulls. The other is planted in the bed beside my shoulder as he looms over me, changing the angle to a deeper one that has me gasping and pleading. I'll say anything for the orgasm he promises.

"Yes."

"I need you like this." He plunges his cock inside me again and again, stealing the breath from my lungs, and the bite of his fist in my hair as he pulls drives me closer to the edge.

"Oh, God," I moan. I try to drop my head down to the bed, but his grip on my hair holds me in place.

"Look at me," Jake commands me, and I turn to look at him, his face just inches from mine.

His thrusts become harder and more erratic, and I feel his cock swell inside me. I'm so close that when he crushes his mouth to mine in a punishing kiss, I cry out as I come. Jake swallows down my cries and follows me over the edge.

He lets go of my hair and drops down farther to cover my body with his larger one. He braces his weight on his hands at either side of my head. When it feels like I can finally catch my breath, he uses his chin to move my hair off my shoulder and places a soft, open-mouth kiss to the back of my neck, sending shivers down my spine.

"Good morning," he says softly, almost shyly,

which is silly in comparison to the carnal way he woke me up.

"Good morning," I whisper back and feel his smile against my skin.

Jake places one more kiss there before slipping free from my body and then lifting me into his arms to carry me into the shower. He does not give me a chance to be shy about what happened between us last night. Instead of worrying about facing him this morning after he made love to me last night, Jake woke me halfway to a climax for the ages and then fucked me hard on my knees. It just goes to show I never know which Jake I have with me at the moment.

I decide those are thoughts for another time when he walks into the water with me in his arms and gently sets me on my feet. I feel the warm spray as it cascades over us, and I close my eyes and enjoy the way it soothes my aching muscles. It's been a long time since I was loved like that in bed. Actually, I'm not sure I've ever been made love to the way Jake did.

I open my eyes when I feel a soft washcloth against my skin and am treated to the sight of Jacob washing my body. He gently cups my pussy for a second, and I look to him and see fire flash behind his blue eyes.

"I'm not gonna lie; I love the look of my cum on your thighs." I had always known there was a rougher side to Jake. That even though he was born of old money, New York stock, he had gone on to the Naval Academy and then earned his way to become a Navy SEAL. What I did not know was how much I would enjoy the dirty words that flow like water from his mouth.

"Hmm," I answer, as I'm unwilling to voice my real feelings right now.

I tip my head back as he massages shampoo into my hair and then rinses it clean. His fingers feel so good on my scalp, and I can't help the moan that slips free from my mouth. I feel his hard cock rise up and brush against my waist, and I open my eyes and reach for him, but he dances out of my grasp.

"I fucked you hard," he says by way of an explanation.

"Yes, you did."

"I shouldn't want you like I do." His voice rumbles against the shower tiles. "But every time I'm near you, my cock is harder than it's ever been, and I can't stay away."

"So don't," I whisper and wonder who this woman is, driven by her baser needs. This isn't me at all. I am cool and clearheaded—*always*. But with Jake, I can't seem to help but jump in feet-first.

"I was too rough with you this morning," he says. "You need time to recover."

"Then let me take care of you," I offer, and before he can answer, I sink down to my knees on the shower floor and take his hard length into my mouth.

"Grace," he rasps. "Fuck, fuck, Grace."

But I don't stop. I twist his length at the base as I pump my fist up and down his shaft while I swirl him as deep into my mouth as I can take him. Jake tunnels his fingers into my hair. He seems to love to grip it, to pull it when he's close to losing his carefully leashed control.

I swirl the tip of him on my tongue before pushing his length all the way to the back of my throat. I hear a little catch of his breath and decide to do it again. He pumps his hips a little as I take him back into my mouth, and I think the move is involuntary, but I love it. I want him to lose control.

"Grace," he rasps when he hits the back of my throat and tries to pull back. "Grace, honey, you have to let me go. I'm going to come."

I feel my eyes widen in triumph and dig my nails into his ass cheeks to pull him farther back into my throat and suck hard. Jake tightens his grip on my hair and spills in my mouth. I swallow him down and wipe the back of my hand against my lips just before he grips me under my arms and hauls me up against his body, slamming his mouth down on mine.

My knees buckle a bit when he lets go of me, and I keep my feet underneath me by nothing less than an act of God. Jake backs under the spray to make quick work of his own shower needs and winks at me. His smile's so happy and carefree that his dimples appear, and I can't help but smile back.

When he's done, he shuts off the water and wraps me in a big, fluffy towel before circling one around his own waist. We part ways to go into our own closets to dress, because the master bedroom in Jake's family heirloom brownstone has his and hers dressing rooms on either side of the master bathroom.

I pull on a pair of panties and a matching bra before dropping a sheath dress over my head. I wrap my hair up in the towel so it won't leave water spots on my dress, but based on Jake's reaction to me this morning, I shouldn't walk around in my underwear when I need to be getting ready for work. There's no need to poke the bear.

I sit down on the padded bench and roll thigh-highs up my legs before padding back into the bathroom to brush my teeth and put on my makeup. I run a round brush through my hair under the dryer and decided to leave it down today.

When I look up, Jake is watching me from the doorway. He's in a perfectly tailored suit and looks ever the popular politician. But his eyes are hungry.

"Don't even think about it," I practically shout as I point at him. "I need food, and then I need to go to work and clear my schedule, so I can hit the campaign trail with you in a few weeks. Otherwise, Rick will bury my body in a cornfield halfway to Iowa," I joke.

"He wouldn't fucking dare."

"I was just teasing," I say, holding my hands up.

"Well, it's not fucking funny," he growls, prowling closer and closer to me. "No one touches what's mine." And then he kisses me like his life depends on it before turning on his heels and stalking out of the room.

I stand there stunned for a minute before turning

back to the mirror to fix my lipstick. And then I slip on my heels and put on my jewelry before heading down the stairs to find my mercurial fake boyfriend but very real lover.

I WINCE AS STARS dance in front of my eyes from the flashes of cameras as we step out onto the front stoop. There are more and more of them out here every damn day. They seem to be multiplying like rabbits.

Once again, Jake is Superman, swooping in to rescue me so videos of me looking like I have a nervous twitch don't end up on the internet. He pulls me in close to him like a man proud to have the woman he loves by his side. It all makes me feel so confused and conflicted.

"Good morning, everyone," he calls out good-naturedly.

"Are wedding bells ringing, Senator?" someone calls out.

"I don't know." Jake laughs. "But when I do, you won't be the first to know!" And everyone laughs.

"Does Ms. Sanders want to marry you?" someone else calls out.

"I don't know the answer to that either. I guess stay tuned."

"Rumor has it she will be hitting the campaign trail with you for the Midwest leg," someone else shouts.

Damn, Rick works fast. I hold in a sigh of frustration before I answer.

"I certainly am," I say with a bright smile. "I can't wait to get out there and support a great guy like Jake."

"Will the senator have your vote?"

"Absolutely."

"One more question!" someone shouts, but Jake is already moving me toward our waiting vehicle.

"If you'll all excuse us," he says, "I need to get my girl to the office."

He ushers me in, and I slide across the bench seat to make room for him. Jake climbs in behind me and shuts the door. It's not until we pull away from the curb that I can finally breathe a sigh of relief.

"It's not so bad, is it?" Jake asks, looking a little concerned. I feel bad he looks so upset on my behalf, and I don't want him to feel bad. What is happening to me that I don't want my sexual nemesis to feel bad? Although, truth be told, he wasn't my arch enemy when he made love to me last night, and he wasn't my arch enemy when I hit my knees for him this morning either. Maybe Jake isn't so bad? And little secret part of me whispers that when he's bad, he is so very good.

"No," I say softly. "It's not so bad. It just always

surprises me."

I look over at him and he seems… upset over it, and I don't know why, but I just can't stand the thought of Jake upset over my reaction to the paparazzi. I am the reason we're in this situation to begin with. A part of me whispers that maybe I'm starting to care for Jacob Chancellor in ways I would have if we hadn't been thrown together. That maybe this is more than just convenience and sex.

"I'm sorry," Jake says thoughtfully. "I think we just have to stay the course."

"Maybe you shouldn't distract me so much," I reply, making a face to make him laugh, and he does.

"I bet I could distract you even better," Jake says after a moment. His mouth is pressed to the shell of my ear. His hand is on my thigh, sneaking under the hem of my dress.

"Jake," I warn. I look at Gus, Jake's Secret Service agent, and Rob, his driver. Both of them are looking straight ahead as if they haven't a care in the world.

"Be very quiet and they'll never know."

By now, the tip of his middle finger grazes the edge of my panties, and he slides it along the leg seam, back and forth, back and forth. The motion is slow and maddening. I try to press my legs together so he can't get his hand closer, but it's no use. I am weak.

He slides a finger under the lace that covers my center and just glides up and down my slit, never penetrating, never touching my clit, just heightening my senses into one brutal point that pulses between my legs.

Jake pulls his hand out from under my dress like it was never there at all, like I imagined the whole thing. And then the door to the car is opening and he's helping me out in front of my office building with a wink.

Stay the course, my ass.

Jacob is turning me into a… a… sex fiend! This is unacceptable.

I spend the whole elevator ride with Jake and Gus thinking how great a sex diet would be. We shouldn't have sex for a while. Sex is bad. Bad, bad, bad, bad, bad. It's clouding my judgement. I would never have let him—or anyone else for that matter—finger me in a car with other people sitting up front. Jake is making me lose my mind.

When we walk down the hall, Carter is there waiting for me with a smile and a cup of coffee. "Morning, boss."

"Good morning, Carter," I say distractedly.

"Mind giving us a few minutes?" Jake asks, and I narrow my eyes on him.

"Sure," Carter responds quietly, and I can tell by the look on his face that I'll have some explaining to do in about twenty minutes. Here's to hoping I can distract him with campaign trail planning talk.

"Don't be mad," Jake says with a rueful smile playing on his sinful mouth. "I'll make it better tonight."

"No, you will not," I reply, and it comes out much sharper than I meant it to. Jake raises one eyebrow in question. I rush to explain. "We have the One Soldier, One Mission Gala tonight."

"Fuck," he bites out, pulling me into his arms. "I forgot. I'm sorry, sweetheart. I'd be happy to put you out of your misery now—"

"Absolutely not," I interrupt, swatting his arm. "I think we need to focus."

"Focus?"

"Y-yes," I stammer under the full weight of his gaze. "We need to focus on our mission. Without getting distracted."

"Distracted?"

What? Is there an echo in here?

"Yes. Distracted. We need to worry more about pulling our bacon out of the fryer and less about sex. Yes?"

"No."

"I'm glad we agree," I tell him as I begin bustling around my office and trying to herd him out the door.

"I didn't agree with you," he says, and there is a funny look on his face. It's like a mix of frustration and amusement.

"What?" I ask, but it ends a little shrill, because he pulls me into his arms again.

"I said I don't agree with you," he explains gently. "We're not going to stop kissing and touching."

"No?" My voice sounds pretty breathless even to my ears.

"No." He smiles, and those twin dimples wink at me and make me go stupid. "And I'm going to make love to you like I did last night."

"Okay."

"And if you run, I'm going to chase you," he says, and his voice is rough like velvet over broken glass.

"Yeah?"

"And then I'm going to fuck you like I did this morning."

I open my mouth to reply, but I don't get a chance, because Jake crushes his mouth to mine, his tongue fighting me for what we both know we need. But I can't help but feel like half of me wants to run toward him and the other half wants to run far, far away.

I stumble a little and have to take a half step back when he lets go of me. And then with a promise to pick me up in enough time for me to get ready for the gala, he leaves me standing there like an idiot as he walks out of my office.

"What the fuck was that?" Carter screeches like a little girl when he rushes in my office and slams the door shut, so we can talk privately. His timing is impeccable. He had to have been watching for when Jake and Gus walked out the door, because as soon as Jake left, here was Carter.

"I'm in love with Jacob Chancellor," I say without

any inflection.

"Well, I know that, silly," he replies. "Is there trouble in paradise?"

"Yes," I whisper.

"Well? What happened?" he practically shouts. "Did you fight? Did he cheat?"

"No," I answer. "No, none of those things."

"Well then, what is it?"

"I think I'm really in love with him. Not 'I was in love with that lobbyist three years ago but wasn't bothered when he fucked that intern at Jules's station on camera,'" I explain. "Like 'if it doesn't work out, I'll be devastated' in love with him."

"Oh, honey," Carter sighs like he's watching a goddamned Hallmark movie. "You found your penguin." If there's one thing Carter loves, it's other people finding their forever person since he found his. Carter is a true romantic.

"Yeah," I say as I burst into tears. "Isn't it terrible?"

He gathers me into his arms and rocks me like a giant baby. When I have finally calmed down, Carter assures me that everything will be all right. He knows how I really am? How I've never made time for another person in my life, how I never thought that I would find love so I never bothered, and worst of all he knew how attracted I always was to Jake even if I never told him all of the sordid details like I did with Jules. Then he tells me my hair and makeup stylist is booked for tonight and that she'll be at the brownstone at five be-cause above all else, he's damn good at his job which is managing me.

"We need to clear the dockets and hand off the cas-es we have," I tell him.

"Why?" he asks.

"We're going campaigning with my penguin," I explain, making him laugh.

"Excellent. I'll coordinate everything with the henchman."

"Thank you."

"Let's go and win your penguin the White House!"

**OUR FAVORITE
SENATOR MAY BE
ON THE OUTS WITH
CAMPAIGN MANAGER.**

THIRTEEN

Fake it till you make it

"**Y**ou have got to be shitting me."

Jake picked me up right at four o'clock, so I wouldn't be late to meet my hair and makeup artist. Cara has been making me look good for formal occasions for the last year and a half, and I like to think we've become pretty good friends in that time.

Cara is a single mom to the prettiest eight-year-old little girl with dark, rich brown hair like her mom's and startling green eyes. She's a couple years younger than Jules and me, but not by much. And as far as I can tell, her baby-daddy has never been in the picture. She has never, not once, ever mentioned an ex to me or Jules.

"Hey, Auntie Grace," Rachel says when I open the door to greet them.

"Hey, kid, what's up with you?" I ask as I tousle her hair, making her laugh.

"Sorry," Cara says when she rolls her tote into the house behind her daughter. "My sitter is sick. I think being sick means she's getting laid."

"Oh the good old days," I say wistfully, making Cara laugh.

"Here," Gus says, taking the heavy tote on wheels from Cara and lifting it into his arms like it's no heavier than a sheet of paper. "Let me take that for you."

"Thanks," she says with a sweet smile.

"Wow," I whisper with my eyes wide. "I think our stoic Gus might be smitten."

"Oh hush, you." She laughs. "Now show me what you're wearing so I can work my magic."

"Right this way, boss." I lead her up the stairs to the master suite, and she whistles as she takes in the palatial digs.

I lead her into the closet and show her the whisper-pink gown with a gold beaded sweetheart neckline and pink flowy skirt that all comes together to be equal parts sexy and sweet.

"Holy hot Cinderella, Batman!" Cara whispers. "I fucking love it."

I'm pairing the dress with my crystal-studded Louboutins and earrings that are big shiny flowers made out of clusters of diamonds. I really pulled out all of the stops for this one. Ironic it's the first time I won't be going to one of these things on my own; instead, I'll be dressed to the nines to be someone else's arm candy. I hold in a sigh, and Cara doesn't seem to notice, as she's lost in her own thoughts.

"Okay," she says suddenly. "I've got it. Let's go set you in rollers."

I follow her into the bathroom, and she brushes out my long blonde hair before wrapping it this way and that in large hot rollers. I have a feeling that when I'm done, I'll look something like a movie star from the forties.

"All right, you know the drill." She laughs as I roll my eyes.

"You just like to see me in my undies," I say.

"Don't you know it. And don't mess up my rollers either."

"I won't," I reply as I step into my closet. I pull on a pair of white lace panties and a matching long-line strapless bra that wraps around my waist and dips low in both the back and front with molded cups to hold up my breasts.

I hustle back into the chair we've pulled into the bathroom and sit back while Cara transforms my face into magic. I love the feel of her brushes on my face as she dusts shimmers and powders here and there.

"I forgot my bowtie," Jake says as he tumbles into the bathroom to see me in my undies with my hair in rollers and Cara applying my makeup. "Holy fuck."

His expletive makes Cara laugh, and I decide to introduce them. "Jake, this is Cara. Cara, this is Jake."

"Hi, Cara," he says, but he never takes his eyes off me, which makes her giggle even harder.

"Can I see you in the closet for a moment?" he asks me, but it's Cara who answers him.

"Absolutely not," she practically shouts, making him jump a little. "If she goes with you, you're going to fuck her and then you'll ruin all my hard work. Fuck her later."

"You don't know that," Jake says. "I could be careful."

"I don't think so, Senator Chancellor." She gives him a sweet smile.

"Jake," he corrects her.

"Jake," she repeats. "I've had a man look at me like that before. I know the look of one who is at the end of his patience."

"Better get that bowtie and run," I say before I bust out laughing.

"Don't think there won't be retribution, Ms. Sanders," he tells me with a twinkle in his blue eyes.

"I would expect nothing less, Senator."

And then he moves to his closet, and Cara and I wait quietly until he gets the accessories he needs and takes them to the spare room where he's dressing.

"Holy shit," Cara says as she fans herself. "Have fun tonight."

"You know I can't stand these things," I tell her as I roll my eyes. The dog and pony shows were never my favorite thing.

"No. I meant after," she corrects with a look to the doorway where Jake just left. "That man clearly has plans for you."

"We'll see."

When she's done with my makeup, she carefully unrolls each of my curls and brushes them this way and that before pinning one side back with a gold barrette. I roll stockings up my legs, and then Cara holds my dress out for me to step into and zips me up.

"Here," she says, handing me the deep-pink lipstick she slicked on my lips, and I drop it into my beaded clutch. "Oh! Your shoes!"

"Right here, Cinderella," Jake says as he holds them out in his hand. I move to reach for them, but instead, he drops to one knee and takes my foot in his hands and slips the heel on me before setting it back on the ground, tapping my other foot to let me know to lift it to his ministrations.

"Thank you."

"And this," he says after he stands and pulls a long velvet box from his coat pocket. He snaps open the box and plucks a gorgeous diamond tennis bracelet from the silk pillow. He unceremoniously chucks the box onto the counter, making me smile and Cara laugh. Jake wraps the bauble around my wrist and then lets me go. "I saw it and thought of you."

"I don't know what to say," I tell him honestly.

"You don't have to say anything at all."

We stare at each other for moments before the spell is broken by Rick shouting the house down.

"Is this some kind of a joke?" he roars.

"What?" I look to Jake, who looks just as confused as I do, but it's when I look at Cara and see her features frozen in fear that the puzzle pieces all start to click into place. "Oh no."

Unfortunately, Rachel chooses that moment to slide into the room on two wheels, totally unaware that you could cut the tension in the room with a knife.

"Hey, Mom!" she calls out happily. She has big headphones over her ears and probably can't hear anything. "Can I have a new game on my phone?"

Cara just stands there stunned.

"Mom?" Rick parrots. I can see the wheels ticking behind his eyes.

Oh fuck, this is not good. This is so not fucking good. Rick and I are on a shaky truce, Jake is feeling very territorial, and Cara is my friend. In my mind I can't rationalize sweet Cara with the brute force of Rick Donnovan.

"I can explain," Cara says, her voice quiet. "But not now."

"Mom?" Rachel asks, suddenly realizing the room is not a friendly one.

"You have got to be shitting me," he bites out.

"How could you? Is this some kind of a sick joke?"

"No," she says adamantly. "No, you know me. I would never do that."

"I don't think I know you at all," Rick hisses before turning on his heels. "This is fucking bullshit."

And then he's gone.

"That was…" Jake trails off as we all think the same thing.

"My husband," Cara says before turning to me. "I think we should be going. I'm so sorry, Grace."

"Don't worry," I tell her. "We'll talk later. It'll be okay."

"I don't know about that," she says before she chews on her thumbnail.

"Why don't you both go to dinner and a movie on me," Jake says. "I think you'll feel better after some fun."

Cara's face goes soft. "That's very kind of you, but I don't know—"

"It's nothing," he assures. "Joe will take you." It's not lost on me that he's assigning a security officer to make sure Rick doesn't lose his ever-loving mind. I don't think he would hurt her, but I'm guessing he's feeling like his whole life is a lie right about now, and I can certainly relate to that. Jake taking care of my friend even though it might be in direct opposite of what his friend would want or need goes a long way to show how good of a man he really is.

And God, I could love him for it.

"Well, shall we?" He holds out his hand to me. Quietly, he leads me to the car. Instead of the usual black SUV that transports us all over town, a black limo waits in its place.

Outside, the press waits to snap pictures of us, and I smile and wave like I'm a princess. I let Jake play my handsome prince as he presses a kiss to my cheek and then leads me to the limo. And all the while, I can't stop thinking that it is fake, fake, fake. Even if it was becoming more, Cara and Rick are a harsh reminder that when it goes bad, it goes very, very bad.

"I have one more thing for you," Jake says with a cheeky grin. His happy mood is contagious, and I think for a second that all my worry was in my head. We're going to be just fine.

And then I look to see another jewelry box sitting in the palm of his upturned hand. But this one is much smaller.

"What's this?" I ask as I stare at the velvet box.

"Go ahead and take it," he says. "It won't bite."

I pluck it out of his hand and snap open the lid. The most gorgeous engagement ring sits nestled in the soft silk pillows. My breath seizes in my lungs, because if I could ever have chosen a ring for me, it would be this one. It has a large Ascher-cut diamond set in platinum, and tiny diamonds of various sizes make up the halo.

Jake takes the ring from the box and slides it onto my finger. It's a perfect fit.

I sit there staring at it on my finger, thinking it's the loveliest thing I have ever seen and that while he didn't actually ask me to marry him, his proposal is very Jake. I think I'll remember this night for the rest of my life. The night a man I am falling in love with hard and fast gave me the most beautiful engagement ring while on our way to a gala. And I'm dressed like Cinder-freaking-ella. If this isn't a fairytale, I don't know what is.

"Rick said the new Gallup polls are showing we've been living together too long for the evangelicals. It was time to put a ring on it." He laughs.

I was wrong. This isn't a fairytale; it's a nightmare.

I'm in love with a man who doesn't love me, and worse yet, I have to marry him.

I smile at him. It feels a little brittle on my face, but that's to be expected. Jake doesn't seem to notice anyway. I can pretend to be the loving fiancée tonight. And tomorrow too. I'll just take it one day at a time.

I guess sometimes you just have to *fake it till you make it*.

Or at least I'll die trying.

A PRINCESS FIT FOR THE SENATOR.

FOURTEEN

I just want you

"It'll never last," the hateful words are whispered in my ear and I hate that part of me knows it's true, while the other half bristles at the idea of ever not belonging with Jake. And above all else, I should have known that this reckoning was coming. How could I have been so distracted?

Jake and I stepped out of the limo to our names being called and camera flashes popping left and right like I had never seen before. And that's saying something, because the crowd that followed us around was growing to a small army's size by leaps and bounds every day.

Jake made sure to always be touching me in some way as we slowly progressed up a step and repeat toward the entrance to the gala. And each move, each brush of his hand on the small of my back or the way he holds me close to him with a strong grip on my hip, each swish of my skirt as it rustles against his tuxedo pants, causes another fissure to tear in my heart, because it was never real, and it was never going to be real. And nothing really slams that point home like the twenty-pound rock weighing down my left hand.

Reporters asked him about the charity we were here to support, and he spoke openly about what his time in the Navy meant to him and how his time in service makes him able to understand what our military goes through every day. It was a great segue into his campaign platforms. I was even drawn into his spell.

Finally, we make it to the door, and Jake is drawn into conversation. He's a popular man, and everyone wants an audience with him. I'm going to use that as an excuse to put a little much-needed distance between us.

"Oh," I say excitedly. "I see an old friend. You'll be all right, won't you, darling?"

Jake narrows his eyes on me like he doesn't quite believe me. I smile a little brighter and hope it doesn't look like a grimace. If ever there was a time I needed him to not see through me, it's now. I'm not ready to admit how I feel about him, not now, and maybe not ever.

"Sure, sweetheart," he says adoringly. He's really laying it on kind of thick, and I want to throw up. He leans into me, and his lips brush the shell of my ear. "Don't be long."

"I won't," I promise, and I'm pretty sure we both know I'm lying through my teeth. And then I excuse myself and make my way to the complete opposite side of the room. I finally breathe a sigh of relief.

Too bad it doesn't last long.

"DANCE WITH ME," JAKE says from behind me. I look over my shoulder and feel my heart pang painfully against my chest at the sight of him. He's too damn handsome for his own good—*or mine*.

"Sure," I answer him. "If you gentlemen will excuse me…"

I reach for Jake's outstretched hand and let him lead me onto the dance floor. He pulls me close into his arms and surprises me with sure footsteps as he waltzes me around the floor.

"Why are you avoiding me?" he growls low in his throat.

"I'm not avoiding you," I answer his question. I look over his shoulder and paste a smile on my face. Everyone is watching. I feel like I'm living in a fish bowl. "I'm doing my job and trying to help you win an election."

"Really?" He raises an eyebrow. I mean, not really. I did talk to our mutual acquaintances about his campaign but really, I was just keeping a little distance between us. Still, I'm not going to admit that out loud. "Grace?"

"Oh, shut up a twirl me, Senator." Jake throws his head back and laughs. He is so beautiful when he allows himself to be free like that. If we had the attention of the room before, now every eye in a twenty mile radius is turn to us and I couldn't care less because as his spins and twirls me around the floor with a gracefulness that I have never expected, Jake makes me feel like we're the only two people in the world.

WHY AM I AVOIDING him again? Oh right, because I love him and he doesn't love me.

Jake has spent the evening dancing with me, making sure I have a glass of champagne when I want one, and holding me close when he has to rub elbows with the who's who of New York. I stay quietly by his side in my role as arm candy. Every now and then, he shoots me a weird look, but I can't decipher it. He should be happy. This is what we were supposed to do.

"I'm going to powder my nose," I whisper in his

ear. "I'll be right back."

"Don't be long," he says as he nuzzles the side of my neck.

"I won't," I whisper before I float off to the ladies' room.

Jake has this way about him where he makes me feel cherished and loved. I have to remind myself of what is real and what isn't. By the time I see to my needs and wash my hands, I have decided to just enjoy what I have while I have it. I pop open my clutch and pull out my lipstick tube. So what if he doesn't feel the same way I do? He's great in bed and makes me feel amazing. Jake is attentive and caring. What more could I want?

I have my mouth open in that weird O-shape women do when they apply lipstick, when a snide voice shakes me from my thoughts.

"It'll never last," Ashley Jeffries sneers as she steps up to the mirror beside me. I blot my lips together and drop my lipstick back in my clutch. "I mean, what could he possibly see in you?"

I don't bother answering. Jakes former lover knows exactly how she feels about the situation, and nothing I do will change that. It's ironic that the second I decide to settle for what he's willing to give me during this fake engagement, she shows up and throws her real relationship with him in my face.

Maybe I should thank her for the reminder.

"Like I said—" She shrugs. "—it won't last long,

so don't get too comfortable in my house."

I pull my compact out of my clutch and pop it open, pulling the little pad out to blot my nose. My giant ring glints in the fluorescent lights of the restroom, and our eyes lock in the mirror when she sees it. Ashley grabs my hand and yanks hard.

"What the fuck is that?" she screeches, and I feel an awful sense of triumph that it's my finger Jake's ring sits on right now.

I snatch my hand back and look away as I drop my compact into my bag and snap it closed. If I was hoping to exit the ladies' room without another word from her, I was sorely disappointed. Unfortunately for me, I know exactly the kind of woman Ashley Jeffries is.

"Like I said, don't get too comfortable," she repeats as she looks me up and down and clearly finds me lacking. "I'll be fucking him by the end of the week."

"Tell him I said hi when you do." I wink and then walk out of the room.

By the time I make it back to Jake, I'm over this evening and my head is pounding. Maybe I should just publish the photos myself and let the chips fall where they may. Then I can walk away from this farce, and Jake can go back to Ashley and all the other women in his life who want to be in his bed regardless of who was there the night before. All I know is I can't be one of them.

"Everything all right?" he asks softly when I make my way to his side.

"I have a headache," I respond. "Champagne always gets to me, but I love it so."

"Well, it was a night to celebrate. It is getting pretty late," he says as he pulls out his phone and sends a text to his driver that we're ready to go. "I should get you home."

"I'd hate to turn into a pumpkin at midnight," I try to joke, but by the look on his face, Jake isn't buying it.

Cameras flash again as we make our way outside to the car. Fuck, I just need a minute. This is ridiculous. Panic claws up my throat at the thought of always being watched—by the media, by my blackmailer, by strangers. People I don't even know having a vested interest in my life. How many of them will cheer like Ashley Jeffries when Jake casts me aside for another? I feel like I'm spinning out of control.

Jake helps me into the dark limo before sliding in beside me. We sit in silence as the car pulls away from the curb. When we're finally a few blocks away, Jake turns to me.

"What's wrong?"

"Nothing." I shrug. "I just have a bit of a headache. It was a long night."

"It was," he agrees. And then he cups my face in his hands and gently forces me to look at him. "But now tell me what's really wrong."

"What are we doing here?" I sigh. "Should we really be faking this relationship any longer?"

"It didn't feel so fake when you were begging for my cock this morning," he says, and I flinch. "Don't do this."

"I'm not doing anything."

"Don't pull away from me." And then he crushes his mouth to mine, and like I always do, my body caves to his demands.

I grip his hair in between my fingers and pull as he thrusts his tongue into my mouth. Jake drops down to the floor to sit on his knees in front of me and pushes down the top of my beautiful dress, my breasts popping free. He kisses and licks and nips his way down my throat and sucks a pink tip into his mouth, and I moan.

I arch my body, desperate for some kind of friction to put out the flames, and he answers me by bunching the skirt of my dress up over my thighs and higher still until he exposes my panties. The ripping sound tears through the air around us, and my panties are gone. Jake shoves them in his coat pocket along with his discarded bowtie.

"You can't deny what we have together," he growls as he runs a fingertip through the moisture at my slit. "You're so wet for me."

"Yes," I admit as he slowly penetrates me with a finger. It's so much and yet not enough. And even sooner, Jake takes it away.

The clank of his belt sounds over our breathing as he unbuckles it and unzips his slacks, freeing his hard cock. Otherwise, he is still completely dressed, and there is something so forbidden, so erotic about that, and it makes me desperate for him.

Jake grips his hard length at the base and closes his eyes. It's the only sign he is as out of control right now as I am.

But it's when he leans forward and opens them, focusing those burning baby blues on me, that my breath seizes in my lungs. I'm not sure what I see there, but I do know there will be no escaping it.

And then he notches the tip of his cock at my entrance and slams home. On instinct, I wrap Jake up in my arms and legs as he pulls almost all the way out and drives into me over and over again.

"Do not run from me," he demands as he pumps harder.

"No," I whisper.

"I will find you." He plunges faster. This will be a hard and fast fuck, and it's what we both need right now. Too many emotions are swirling too close to the surface.

"Yes."

"And I will fuck you until you forget why you ran in the first place." Oh fuck, fuck, I'm so close. This wild, primal way Jake commands me, owns me, has me spiraling higher and higher.

"Jake," I plead.

"You're mine."

"Yes," I pant and cling even tighter to him.

"Say it," he demands as his movements become more erratic.

"I'm yours," I cry out, and then I come, with Jake following me over the edge.

We cling to each other as our hearts continue to beat faster than normal, his cock still planted deep inside me, connecting us in the most intimate of ways. When he pulls out, I miss him. He tucks himself back into his slacks and does up his belt. Jake looks as if nothing is out of the ordinary for him, and I look like a disheveled mess.

He follows my gaze to look down at me, my breasts exposed with little red love bites peppered all over them. My dress is hiked up over my thighs where streaks of his cum begin to dry, and my panties are long gone. The look of male pride in his eyes is ridiculous and intoxicating. Even after everything, I still want him, and what does that say about me?

Jake swipes his fingertips through the combined moisture between my legs and gently wipes it over the tops of my thighs again and again. My mind goes back to this morning when he said he likes to see his cum on me. He dips his middle finger inside me, and I bite my lip to keep from calling out, from begging him for more. And then he takes that finger and traces my lower lip with it. It smells of me and him and sex and sin, and I swipe at it with my tongue. Jake follows the movement with his eyes before crushing his mouth to mine. But the kiss is over much too soon, and he's tucking my sensitive breasts back into my dress and smoothing my hair from my face.

"We're home."

A FAIRYTALE ENDING IS SURE TO BE NEAR.

FIFTEEN

Consequences

The front door snicks closed behind me, the sound deafening in the quiet house. Something changed between us in the car on the way home, and I don't know what or how.

I glance at him over my shoulder. The sight of Jake in his tux with his collar open at the neck displaying his tanned skin takes my breath away. We're not together, but we're not apart either. I'm so confused, and at the same time, I'm so drawn to him.

He takes a measured step toward me, and then another and another.

"Jake," I whisper.

He scoops me up in his arms like the bride I'm pretending to be, like I'm cherished and loved, and strides purposefully up the stairs. He doesn't stop until he's standing beside the bed. Jake slowly lowers me down his body to stand before him. His eyes never leave mine.

I watch with rapt attention, barely blinking as he lets his suit jacket slide down his arms, and then he tosses it to the padded bench that sits at the foot of the bed before reaching for me. He guides me without words to turn around. He deftly tucks his fingers into the top of my dress and lowers the zipper, letting the material part and fall to the floor where it pools around my feet.

Jake scoops me up in his arms and drops me to sit on the edge of the bed while he picks up my princess dress like it's the most precious thing in the world and not an overpriced hunk of material. Carefully, he lays it down on the padded bench over his jacket before prowling back around to the side of the bed to stand before me.

There's something about the arms of a man as the tendons and muscles tighten and flex as he unbuttons his cuffs. Jake is no different. His strong fingers flick each stud open one by torturous one then down the front of his pristine white shirt before the blessed material finally parts and he shrugs the garment off, letting it fall to the floor.

I feel the heat coming off his muscular chest and arms in waves as he reaches around me and flicks open the hooks holding my strapless bra closed, leaving me sitting here in nothing but my Cinderella Louboutins. Jake takes a half step back and watches me from under hooded eyes as he opens his belt and unzips his slacks. He toes off his dress shoes and socks before pushing his black boxer briefs down his legs with his pants.

His cock stands long and tall from his body, and I lean forward, placing a kiss to the very tip of him. He lets out a rough rumble from deep in his chest and tunnels his fingers in my hair. His reaction turns me on, and I reach for him, wrapping my hand around his shaft. I place soft, open-mouth kisses to the underside of him and the tip again before slowly taking him into my mouth. I hum as I lick and suck the salty taste of him, while a burning need grows stronger between my legs.

Jake's eyes glow brightly as he watches me. He watches my cheeks pinken and my nipples tighten, my obvious reaction to his pleasure. And then his eyes dip down to where his hard length disappears into my mouth over and over again, and he swells so much that my jaw aches, but I don't want to stop. It's when my hips give an involuntary swivel on the bed, seeking a little relief of my own, that he slips from mouth and tosses me farther up the mattress like I weigh nothing at all.

"You like it, don't you?" he rumbles as he grabs one of my ankles and plucks my heel from my foot, tossing it over his shoulder like it didn't cost three thousand dollars.

"What?" I ask. My voice is breathy and needy. *I'm* needy. I need Jake to put out the fire he lights in me.

"You get off on me and my pleasure," he clarifies

as he chucks my other very expensive shoe to the floor. "Are you hot from sucking my cock, Grace?"

"Yes," I whisper as he climbs up the bed. My legs fall open for him to settle in between them, but he stops short, denying me what I want most.

"If I touched your pussy right now, would you be wet for me?" He sits back on his knees and waits for my answer, even though the evidence of my arousal is currently on display for him to see for himself.

"Yes."

"That's my girl," he praises as he leans forward and braces himself on one arm as he looms over me. He runs the tip of his cock up and down my seam over and over again, letting it dip in just the tiniest bit and then pulling back out. I let out a whimper, because I want it so much.

And then he slides all the way in.

I let out a hiss as he fills me, as he stretches me. I don't think I will ever get used to the feeling of Jake's much larger body as he masters my much smaller one. And I hope I never do.

I rock my hips to meet his as he slowly pulls out to the tip and then glides back in. I rake my nails down his shoulders and then smooth them back up again as he sets a leisurely pace of slip and slide between us.

I feel like a dam about to burst, and Jake acts like he has all the time in the world.

"Faster," I plead.

"No." He continues to stoke the slow-building burn inside me.

"Please," I beg. I scratch at his shoulders and then grip them tight in my hands.

"No." Oh, God, I need him to hurry, before I burst into flames. "You had a fast fuck in the car, and now I want slow."

"It's too slow," I babble. "Baby, it's too slow. I need… *I need.*"

"I know what you need," he says as he wraps my legs around his waist and pushes up so he's sitting on his knees again with my ass in his lap. This new angle pushes him deep, and I have to bite my lip to keep from crying out. "And I'll give it to you."

My head and shoulders are the only parts of me touching the bed now as my body arches back like a rainbow from where he holds me around his hips. He holds me suspended, the push and pull of his cock the only thing keeping me tethered, and he moves faster, pumps harder into my waiting body.

"Yes," I pant, and the knowing smirk on his face would usually annoy me, but right now, I am so close it's clearly deserved.

Jake swirls his hips and drives up into me again and again. I couldn't stop the climax that barrels down on me if I tried, and I twist the sheets in my hands at my sides and fall over the edge.

He drops my backside to the bed and follows me down, never skipping his stride as he thrusts harder and harder before he plants himself deep and calls out my name as he comes.

He glides slowly in and out as exhaustion sweeps over me. I can barely keep my eyes open, so I don't. I let them fall closed and snuggle into Jake's arms as he turns slightly to the side so he's not squishing me. He touches a fingertip to the apple of my cheek. The gesture is so sweet and tender that words I know I shouldn't say slip out of my mouth.

"I think I'm in love with you," I whisper just before I fully succumb to sleep.

I'll worry about the consequences tomorrow.

"WAKE UP, HONEY," JAKE says softly as he kisses my bare shoulder where it peeks above the blankets.

"No," I grumble. "I don't wanna."

I feel his mouth spread in a smile against my skin. "You have to, sweetheart."

"No. It's Saturday," I explain while keeping my eyes closed, but it's too late; I'm awake. That rat. "Hi."

"Hi, honey." He smiles at me.

"Why am I awake?" I ask sleepily.

"Because we have to talk," he answers. I don't like the look on his face, and I know without a doubt what comes out of his mouth I am not going to like.

"I'm sure whatever is bothering you will be just fine," I say, patting his cheek, and trying to avoid the conversation. Whatever it is, whatever is going on with us, I'm not sure I could take an "it's me, not you" talk first thing on a Saturday morning.

"Last night, I went through your stuff in the bathroom, looking for a makeup wipe to clean your face off."

"Okay…?" I hedge. I'm not sure what a makeup remover wipe could lead to for such a serious conversation first thing in the morning.

"And there was something I noticed you didn't have."

What? What don't I have? Fake lashes? Lip brushes? Q-tips? What did I forget to pack? He decides not to leave me hanging, because he answers, rocking my world to the core in the process.

"Sweetheart, I didn't find any birth control pills. And I looked. Grace, are you protected?"

No. The answer is no, I'm not protected. They were making me crazy and giving me headaches. I haven't had a lover in some time, and even when I did, I always used a condom. So not only am I not protected against pregnancy, I'm going out on a limb and guessing I'm also the dumbest chick on the planet for being swept along in the tide of Jake-induced lust.

"No," I whisper and have to stop and clear my throat. "No, I'm not. I didn't—"

"I know," he interrupts me. I wouldn't do something so stupid on purpose. "But honey, I've taken you a lot, and we've never once used a condom."

I wince. "I'm sorry."

"Grace, you have nothing to be sorry about. This is all on me." God, why is he being so nice? "I'm here with you no matter what."

I mentally count on all my fingers. I'm good. I think I'm good. "I think I'm okay. I don't think it's the right timing."

"Well, keep me posted," he says gently. "And when the timing is right, we'll go from there."

"I think we should just go ahead and say the timing is not right, right now," I murmur, making Jake smile his real smile, dimples and all.

"Message received, sailor." Jake drops a quick kiss to my lips, and I let out a breath, thankful we made it through all of the awkward conversations for this morning. "Now, do you want to repeat what you said to me last night?"

I tick through in my brain all the things I might have said last night and can't think of anything super important. I mean, I clearly didn't have the "we should be using NASA-engineered condoms" conversation, so nothing life-altering happened... unless...

No, I couldn't have said it. I was tired, exhausted

really, and overwhelmed with life. I went to sleep after Jake made love to me again, and that was it. But a secret part of my brain whispers it wasn't a dream that I admitted I'm falling for him out loud.

Well, shit.

"Nope, nothing to report here," I lie through my teeth with my eyes wide.

"All right, I'll let you make that play… for now," he says before pressing his mouth to mine in a kiss that sweeps me away. I cling to his shoulders until he pulls back and looks in my eyes. "But if you feel like issuing an audible, I'm all ears."

"I have no idea what you're talking about."

The look Jake gives me says we both know I'm lying, but it's okay for now. Instead, he kisses that spot behind my ear that drives me wild while he settles between my legs, pushing them apart as he lays over me, belly to belly. The feeling of his hard length pressed against my pussy hot and hard but also unmoving has me squirming beneath him to relieve some pressure.

"Is there something you want, Grace?" Jake asks me as he pulls back ever so slightly to glide the underside of his cock through my wetness and grind against my clit.

"Yes, dammit." I close my eyes and try and arch my body against his for a better angle but until Jake lets me, it's no use.

"What's that?" He repeats the move, and I feel like I might die.

"You."

And then he pulls back just enough to line up the very tip of him and slide all the way in. We both groan at the feel of our connection.

"I want you too," he says as he pulls back and plunges back in. It's a steady push and pull. There are not fancy moves this morning, just a primal joining of him and me. "You can tell me when you're ready."

No, I won't. I can never tell Jacob Chancellor that I am in love with him. Never again.

He takes my hands in each of his and holds them on either side of my head as he moves in and out of my body, leading us both to the climax that waits at the end. It washes over me wrapped up in his arms safe and sound, and I love every bit of it as much as it kills me. Jake pulls out at the last moment, and hot ropes of his cum splash across my belly.

He heard me. The fact that Jake hears me, he sees me for who I really am and continues to stay, does heady things to me. It only drives that love deeper into my chest.

"I'll wait until you're ready to say them," he says with all the confidence in the world as he leads me to the shower.

What he doesn't say is that he loves me too.

Life's a real bitch like that.

LIFE WITH THE
SENATOR HAS GONE
TO THE DOGS.

SIXTEEN

Halo

"You're beautiful," Jake says when I finally make my way into the kitchen.

"Thank you." I shyly brush a lock of hair back that's come free from my messy bun.

After we showered, Jake threw on a pair of well-worn jeans and a black T-shirt before pulling a hoodie that had "NAVY" stitched across his chest over it, declaring he was going to make a pot of coffee as he padded out of the room in his bare feet. And why are bare feet sexy? So I followed his lead and pulled on my favorite pair of jeans, the really stretchy kind that feel more like leggings than jeans but make your backside look really good too, a light-blue long-sleeved T-shirt with a scooped neck and tugged on my favorite NYU crew neck over it. I did light makeup in soft, shimmery pinks and nudes and dried my hair before twisting it up on top of my head in a messy bun with a few strategically placed pins. It's a cute weekend look, but it's nothing in comparison to the knockout he brought home last night. It's not beautiful, but it'll do.

I pour myself a cup of coffee and notice for the first time there is a big, fluffy cat sitting in Jake's lap like he belongs there, while Jake happily drinks his coffee and reads his email on his phone. My life is so weird. I feel less like Cinderella and more like Alice when she fell down the rabbit hole.

"So, what's on tap for today?" he asks me.

"I usually go to the animal shelter and help out there for a bit, and then I go check on the Open Arms project. Then I have a date with Jules afterward." While our standing date is for every other Saturday, Jules had sent me a text yesterday asking if we could double down on our weekend plans. I think it's her way of wanting to check in since my life seems to be moving along at warp speed these days.

"That sounds like a solid plan to me," he says as he gently sets the cat on the floor and drops his mug in the sink. "Do we change before dinner or is it burger casual?"

"You're coming too?" I ask and cringe at the hopeful tone in my voice.

Jake smiles gently and nods. "Yeah, I'd like to spend the day with you."

"Okay." I'm not sure what to make of this. This sweet, almost shy side of Jake. Like all of the other pieces that he's shown me—the good and the bad—I like them.

"Let me grab my shoes and my wallet, and we can head out," he says before he presses a quick kiss to my mouth then he leaves the room. My life is so weird.

"NO." I FOLD MY arms across my chest and try and fail to look as stern as possible.

"Please?" Jake whines—yes, he whines. "I love him. He can go for runs with me in the morning, because we all know you are not a morning person."

"I know," I agree because I'm not a morning person. And who freaking jogs anyways? Crazy people and former Navy SEALs, that's who. "That's why I stick to cats. They like naps."

"Sarge might like naps too." Sarge does not look like he takes naps. Sarge looks like he rips the faces off of terrorists for fun and that's putting it mildly.

There was a lot of commotion in the animal shelter when Jake and I walked in. Not just because he's the sexy man about town he is, but because there was a retired police dog who, if they couldn't get him to perk up, they were going to have to euthanize. Apparently,

Sarge's officer, the only one he ever had in his six-year-long career, was killed in the line of duty. They tried to reassign him, but he was too bonded with his partner and had fallen into a deep doggie depression.

Sarge was eventually turned over to this shelter to see if someone between them and Purple Paws could rehabilitate him, but it was no use. He wanted to follow his human across the rainbow bridge. That is, until Jake walked in.

We then learned Sarge's partner had the same tone of voice and cadence as Jake. He also had a similar build and carried himself in the same manner, as he was a soldier with the 101st before he was an NYPD officer. A truer hero there never was.

The minute Sarge heard Jake and I playfully bickering about the cats that he swears he doesn't even like which is a complete and total lie, he perked up. The minute he saw Jake walk past his kennel, he claimed him as his human. And who was I to stand in the way of a true bromance? So somehow, I'm going to have to explain to eight very spoiled felines that they now share their domain with a ninety-pound German Shepherd. A German Shepherd who used to love running six miles a day with his partner.

I sure hope Gus likes dogs.

"Careful, Jake," I wink at him. "Your halo is showing."

"Just don't tell the others," he laughs. "But I'll show you anything you'd like."

I roll my eyes at him but smile anyway. "Oh fine. Welcome to the family, Sarge."

"Hooyah!" Jake shouts as Sarge lets out a bark.

They thankfully loan us a leash and a collar, although Sarge is impeccably trained. We load him up in the SUV to the surprised looks of Gus and Joe.

"If you could please take us to a pet store, that would be great," Jake says politely.

Joe drives us to the nearest pet superstore, and I follow behind the boys while they look at everything. The manager is more than happy to help Jake find everything he could ever need for Sarge. We have bowls and food, leashes and collars, but the best part is watching Sarge check out all the toys. As a working dog, his options were limited, but as a retiree, his life is wide open, and his new human is going to make his remaining years beautiful; I can just tell.

When Sarge finally chooses a pink stuffed octopus that squeaks and a tennis ball, we head back to the car after paying for all of the accoutrements Jake needs for his new furry bestie. I might have even excused myself to cry in the bathroom, because I'm apparently a crier now.

We head to Open Arms, where I get to walk Jake and Sarge around and show them all the facility will do when it's finally open.

"This is fucking amazing," he says after we walk through one last time, and Jake meets all the on-site personnel and thanks them all one by one.

My phone rings as we load Sarge up into the SUV and head home. I pull it out of my bag and see it's Jules.

"Hey, girl," I answer. "Can we have an impromptu night in instead of out?"

"Yeah, but why?" she asks.

"Because Jake just adopted a retired police dog, and I don't want to just dump him in the house with all the cats and bail. Pizza and wine in? I know where Jake hides the good stuff." My offer makes him laugh, and I know Jules hears it too when she answers.

"And where will the good senator be?"

"With us at home," I explain before rolling my lip into my mouth and biting down.

"A casual night at home with the senator everyone wants to interview?" she asks, and I can hear the wheels spinning. "Now that's an offer I can't pass up."

"Take off your press hat," I demand. "This is strictly a friends dinner. Jake is off limits."

"Is he now?" she prompts.

"He is."

"Now this, I can't wait to see." And with that, she ends the call.

"Should I be worried?" Jake asks. "I didn't realize you were besties with the shark of Eagle News."

"Jules?" When he nods, I explain, "Oh yeah, I've known Jules since freshman year at NYU. She's a shark all right, but she's loyal to a fault. She'd take a bullet for me and vice versa."

"Good to know," he says before turning back to hug his new dog for the remainder of the ride home.

When we pull up out front, cameras snap and click. Jake climbs out of the SUV and holds his hands up until everyone stops moving.

"Hey, all," he begins. "I'm going to ask you not to take pictures right now. And I know it's your job and how you put food on the table for your families, but it's for an important reason. Today, Grace and I met and fell in love with a retired NYPD K-9 officer at the shelter where she volunteers. His name is Sarge and his partner was Juan Garcia, the officer who gave the ultimate sacrifice last month here on our own streets.

"Sarge was not doing good, friends. He was going to be euthanized, because he no longer wanted to be in this world without Juan. But somehow, he decided it would be okay to go on with me.

"Now, I don't know how he will react to the media yet, so let's play it by ear. Please. For Sarge?"

When Jake is done speaking, I notice a few are wiping their eyes, but everyone is quiet and all cameras have been put away. Jake escorts Sarge and me up the steps and into the house. He drops a quick kiss to my lips before changing direction again.

"Order some pizzas, please?"

"Sure."

And then he turns on his heels and walks back

out the open door, where Sarge and I stand watching him as he slips his phone from his jeans pocket. Jake starts asking for the names and contact info of every paparazzi who honored his wishes for Sarge with the promise of an interview opportunity when Sarge is ready. Everyone leaves with a smile on their face. And I now know why he is going to be the best president. Jake managed to take a tense situation and turn it into something everyone could live with.

Jules arrives in jeans, a T-shirt with a leather jacket over it, and heels just before the pizza delivery kid, who looks a little starstruck at her. She is always dressed to the nines, but that's just her. She never judges me for my love of casual Saturdays.

Jake takes the pizza into the den and sets it on the coffee table while Jules and I follow behind him.

"I'll give you two a minute to talk about how awesome I am in the sack while I go grab some wine from the cellar," he says on a wink with a smile, flashing his dimples.

"Shit," she says when he leaves the room. "That smile is lethal in person."

"Tell me about it," I droll.

"No, you tell me all about it," she says. What the hell happened?"

"I'm in love with him."

"I can see that," she hisses. "It's plain as the nose on your face. Is he really good in bed or was it just talk?"

"He's the best." I sigh.

"Then what the hell are you complaining about then?"

"Did you not hear the part where I said I was in love with him?"

"And he's clearly in love with you," she says gently.

"Ugh. No, he's not, and it's terrible," I admit, burying my face in my hands.

"What's going on, Grace?"

"Everything," I answer as I wipe my face on the sleeve of my sweatshirt. "It's all a lie… or at least it was. Now, I think I'm really falling for him."

"What? You're not making any sense. I think you better start at the beginning."

"You're right," I agree. "I'm just so mixed up about everything. I don't even know where to start."

"The beginning is usually the best spot," she says gently.

"The Monday after our dinner, an unmarked package was left for me at my office. It held pictures of Jake and I in Clear that looked, well, compromising."

"In Clear?" she asks me. "So you did go talk to him?"

"Not on purpose, no. I was going to walk past him and give him the cold shoulder but my heel caught on a freaking dessert spoon that someone had dropped and he caught me before I could hit the ground."

"Well, that was chivalrous of him," Jules adds.

"With his hand on my ass and his face on my neck," I say pointing to the side of my neck and accidentally drawing attention to the pink marks he left there earlier.

"That is some fantastic beard burn you're sporting today," she laughs.

"This isn't funny," I admonish, but really it kind of is so I give her a goofy smile.

"My apologies. Do go on." She waves her hand like the Queen.

"These pictures could ruin my reputation, his isn't fantastic, or it wasn't at the time."

"You've done well to clean him up," she agrees.

"So, I called him, hating every minute of it," I press on. "Jake said we should meet at a hole in the wall place he likes to go to. He said he could solve all of our problems if I just married him."

"And you agreed."

"I did but the whole time, I kept thinking it was fake and it would end as soon as he was elected," I admit. "But…"

"But the sex is real and so are your feelings," she finishes for me.

"Yeah and it really stinks."

"Grace, I don't think you have anything to worry about here," Jules says softly. She's always thought the most of me and usually she's correct. I'm smart, I'm funny, and I'm the whole package, but now she's completely wrong. A man like Jake Chancellor won't settle down. Sure, he will for a while, but then he'll rip my heart out. A leopard can't change their spots.

"I wish you were right," I whisper as tears pool in my eyes again.

"Honey, I know they covered a lot at NYU and that fancy law school of yours—"

"Harvard," I add helpfully.

"Yes, that," she says as she rolls her eyes. "So you should know that a man like sexy Senator Jake doesn't give a woman what has to be a family heirloom like the one on your ring finger if he doesn't love her."

I look at my hand and remember his less than romantic proposal, and I wince. "It's probably a good fake. We're only engaged because of the optics."

Jules has the audacity to throw her beautiful head back and laugh.

"That's not a fake," she says on a smile. "I would know. And my optics tell me that man is crazy about you."

Just then, I hear footsteps coming up the stairs from the basement.

"Well that man is coming back now, so be quiet," I grit out.

"We're not done here."

"Yes, we are," I growl before pasting a smile on my face just in time as Jake walks back in the room.

"I heard Grace promise you the good stuff, so I figured I'd get the really good stuff out," he says as he drops two bottles on the coffee table and pulls a bottle opener from his jeans pocket.

"I like you," Jules says unceremoniously.

"I like you too," he replies, gifting her with his megawatt smile again.

"Jesus," she says. "That should be registered with the state. How do you keep your panties dry?"

"I don't." I shrug, making Jake laugh.

"To be fair, I just rip them off anyway, so the point is moot," he admits.

"And I am officially jealous," she sighs. "Feed me pizza and wine so I can drown my sorrows."

"Something tells me you are perfectly fine just the way you are, Julia Fairchild," Jakes appraises.

"Right you are, Senator." She winks. "So, I hear you went to Open Arms today after conning the cat lady into taking on a dog."

The dog in question looks up at Jules lovingly when she pinches off a bite of sausage for him.

"It's amazing," he says after taking a bite of his own pizza. "What made you decide to help veterans?" He looks at me.

"Why wouldn't I?" I ask him. "Everyone needs a hand sometimes. Just because they are some of the bravest people in the world doesn't mean they don't need or deserve a helping hand every now and then like anybody else. So to answer your question though, it started with the Purple Paws dogs from the shelter and went from there. The more I learned, the more I wanted to do to help. No one should feel so low that they want to take their own life."

"Thank you," he says when he clears his throat. "It means a lot to me."

"I can see that," I reply softly.

"I had a friend in Bud/s and he just couldn't take it," he explains. "No one knew he was suffering until he wasn't anymore."

"I'm so sorry," I tell him.

"It was a long time ago."

"So what made you choose the Naval Academy?" Jules asks, doing her best to change the subject.

"It pissed off my dad." He laughs.

"Oh dear," I mumble.

"My dad always wanted me to go to an Ivy League school, so I could be the best politician ever. But I really wanted to be a SEAL. So when I was granted a football contract to the Naval Academy, I took it knowing full well I would have a military contract to serve when I was done playing ball."

"That's impressive, Senator," Jules says, and I couldn't agree more.

He shoots her a self-deprecating smile. "I'm not that noble," he says. "I got what I wanted out of it and the added bonus to make my dad mad. But I still had to come home when my contract was up and join the family business. I'm just lucky Rick came too."

"Speaking of Rick," I segue. "Have you heard from him?"

"He'll be all right. He just needed to lick his wounds," Jake says cryptically as he eyes Jules. He is obviously not wanting to divulge too much in case tonight really isn't off the record. "There's a history there between him and Cara."

"I got that. Why didn't you tell me when she got here yesterday?"

"I had never met her before," he explains. "And you didn't tell me her last name was Donovan. How was I supposed to know?"

"That's true."

"Well, I think it's time for me to go," Jules says.

Jake and I show her to the door before we clean up the den and then climb the stairs. We undress each other before climbing into bed, where he once again, make loves to me until I fall apart in his arms before I fall asleep feeling safe and cared for, even if not loved. Things with Jake feel good and real, even if they're not real at all.

Sarge falls asleep on his brand-new dog bed by the window and has happy doggie dreams.

And we did all of this not knowing the end was near. Again, I'm so fucking stupid.

BELLS ARE RINGING FOR A CERTAIN *IT* COUPLE.

SEVENTEEN

Smitten

Pain sears through my body before focusing on one point of contact, and I hold my breath until spots dance before my eyes. I suck in a sharp breath through my teeth, and then the pain dissipates before it is inflicted again from a new area.

"We can no longer be friends, Cara," I grit out.

"For Christ's sake," she snaps. "Quit being such a big fucking baby. You're not the one whose ex-husband is lurking around somewhere in this house. And having to travel for work with him later this week." And she's not wrong. Rick is somewhere in this house with Jake. They're probably drinking beer and eating pizza and not being tortured by their friends.

"How are you doing with all that?" I ask. I try and take a good look at here to see if she look like she's really alright but my eyes won't stop watering so I can't see anything clearly.

"It is what it is," she sighs. "We'll figure out how to be professional."

And then she rips off another strip.

"I've decided that you're fired," I tell after I try and fail to catch my breath.

She laughs, and Goddammit I want to rip her hair out until she's baldheaded.

Riiipppp! She yanks off another cloth strip from somewhere on my body. I don't even know from where anymore. When Cara came over early this morning to prep for the engagement pictures of the century, I thought it might be a soak in the bath and a face mask, maybe some mani/ pedi action. Not waterboarding and bamboo shoots shoved under my fingernails before all of my body hair was ripped out by the roots.

"I think this violates the Geneva Convention."

"You're ridiculous." She rolls her eyes. "What you need is a gag."

"Don't you dare!"

"That was the last one, you candy ass," she says before taking a rough scrub brush, dipping it in a sugar scrub, and applying it to my entire body while I lay on a foldup massage table covered in white towels. And by apply, I mean scrape off a layer or two of my skin.

She applies a less abrasive one to my face then takes washcloths and runs them under warm water to wipe it all off before using a dry, fluffy towel to dry my body. When all is said and done, Cara brushes rich lotion onto my skin and then wraps me up in a big, fluffy robe that dwarfs me, but I don't care. I'm no longer being ripped apart. Don't get me wrong; I love good-quality primping, but this wasn't primping. This was North Korea level torture.

She gives me a light snack of cheese and apple slices with a big bottle of water. I narrow my eyes on the light meal.

"Do you really want to have pizza-face skin and a big bloated belly in pictures that will be on every media news outlet by four o'clock tomorrow afternoon?" she asks me on a raised brow.

"No," I sigh before nibbling on an apple slice.

I sit patiently like a good girl while Cara wraps sections of my hair around a big barrel curling iron and then rolls them up on my head in big loops she secures with pins. When she's done with my hair, she files and paints my nails in a soft nude.

She applies more makeup than I would wear on a normal Tuesday, but it's beautiful, classic. Soft pink blush highlights my cheeks, and my eyes are accentuated with smoky taupes and shimmery nudes. She swipes a soft pink on my lips and the look is perfect.

Cara hands me a black velvet box. I snap it open and see two huge diamond solitaire earrings set on gold posts. They perfectly match the diamond bracelet Jake gave me last week. My heart beats a little faster. I can't believe he's given me another lavish gift. Even though I enjoy the finer things, I'm not the kind of girl to expect them from a lover. If someone buys me jewelry, it's probably me. But Jake has this way of making me feel special when he gives me gifts. That is, until he doesn't. I'm still smarting from the fake engagement, and an ugly voice in the back of my brain asks how many of his former paramours are walking around the tri-state area with diamond bracelet consolation prizes.

I slip the earrings through my ears, and she wraps the bracelet around my right wrist so my engagement ring is the only thing on my left hand. And then she hands me a bagful of under garments. I look at them and then look back at her, unsure if she's playing a joke on me.

"Is this really what you want me to put on?" I ask.

"Yes, why?"

"Because these belong to a kindergarten teacher?"

"No." She laughs. "Just put them on."

I step into a plain pair of nude briefs and tuck my breasts into a matching bra. The most exciting part is the nude thigh-highs I roll up my legs; otherwise, the entire look is awful.

"I have it!" Carter shouts as he runs into the room with a garment bag held up high. "I have the dress!"

"Oh my God," Cara squeals. "Let me see it!"

He loops the hanger over the back of the door and unzips the bag. And I stop breathing. The dress is black with a crew neckline and long sleeves. It would be demure if the entire top wasn't completely sheer except for strategically placed sprays of vines stitched with tiny gold beads. The skirt is sold but is row after row of vertical black ruffles that flow like tiny waves.

"Help me, Carter," Cara says. "It's going to take both of us to get it on her."

And it does. In the end, I just stand there like a mannequin while they push and pull the fabric to coax it into the right place before they do up the invisible zipper. It fits like a glove. Like it was custom made for me. I stare at myself in the full-length mirror while Cara bustles around me, unpinning my hair and smoothing it into soft waves like it was the other night but better.

"Now the shoes," Carter says before popping the lid off a brand-new Louboutin box. They are nude, sky-high pumps with a pointed toe and a skinny strap that crosses the top of the foot.

"You speak my love language, Carter."

"Not me, Senator Chancellor."

Jake, who always pays attention, who always sees me before I see it myself, realized I favor a very expensive brand of designer heels and bought me a pair. I'm not sure what to make of this situation that has become my life. I should just say thank you and move on, but I can't help feeling like the other shoe is about to drop.

Instead of asking the important questions, I slip on my new shoes and head down the stairs to take some fabulous fucking engagement pictures. Jake is waiting for me at the bottom of the stairs in a dark-blue suit with a white shirt underneath and the collar open at the neck.

He's looking at something on his phone, but when Rick says my name and nods in my direction, Jake looks up, and the world just seems to stop. He tucks his phone in his pocket and makes his way to me.

"You are beautiful," he says when I hit the bottom step.

"Thank you. For everything."

"It was nothing," he replies.

"The photographer is here," Rick calls from the entryway.

Jake and I decided we wanted to take pictures out back in the small garden that is attached to the property. Sarge waits for us. He has been brushed and washed and looks handsome as ever. The photographer has us walk through the trees side by side. She poses us on a path, looking like we've been caught in a romantic clinch, when she definitely arranged us that way. And then last, a set of formal poses where we are sitting on the brick steps leading up to the house with Sarge by our sides. I love all of it, but I think the last one will be what gets sent to the different news outlets.

We look perfect in every way.

LOOKS LIKE
LOVE IS IN THE
AIR FOR
AMERICA'S
FAVORITE IT
COUPLE.

EIGHTEEN

Be real

"**C**ongratulations!" another well-wisher greets me. I'm not sure who most of these people are. Friends and family of Jake's, I guess.

By the time the weekend rolled around, our engagement had been the talk of every news outlet in the country and some overseas as well. People wanted to know if it was love at first sight or if it was a shotgun wedding. They wanted to know if I was his mistress when he was with Ashley. That one bothered me more than it should, but whatever.

This last-minute engagement party for the ages was the evil brainchild of Rick and Jake's dad. I'm not entirely comfortable being the center of attention, but it is what it is. I should have known when I asked Jake for help all those weeks ago, it would cost me the life I previously lived. In for a penny, in for a pound, I guess.

It's a lovely event. Smaller than I would have thought they were capable of organizing. Only those important enough to be invited were, to the small-ish event at Tavern on the Green. I am surprised to see the partners from my firm here. That was nice of the senior senator to invite them, even if I basically don't work there anymore. They greet me politely, if not a little distantly, before moving on. I shrug it off. I would probably come to an event like this to meet an infamous senator as well.

The invitee who surprises me most is Mark Jeffries, Ashley's father. The thing about New York elite is that they all know each other. I wonder if it gets old being surrounded by the same small group of people all the time. Thank God I have Jules and Cara and Carter, or I would go absolutely mad. Although, I have never been part of the elite. I have always been on the outside, elbowing my way in or hidden in the trenches, cleaning up their messes. I'm not sure I appreciate this new status update. Either way, I can't help but take in the people in this room and wonder if one of them was the person who tried to ruin me. Are they still out there, waiting for their pound of flesh? Half the people in this room, I've saved from near disaster, and the other half I've beaten the pants off of in the courtroom. It's hard to tell. It could be anyone.

"Good evening, Mr. Jeffries," I greet him when he steps in front of me after the last person I was talking to steps away. He smiles tightly and presses his mouth into a thin line. It's like he's trying to hold back his self-entitled sneer and is struggling under its weight. I see he and his daughter share several charming qualities.

"Let's not waste time here with small talk," he says to me, his voice low and biting. "How much will it take?"

"Excuse me?"

"What's your price?" he pushes.

I can't imagine what he's asking about. Why is he at my engagement party if he doesn't even like me? The questions bounce around in my head like a pinball.

"I'm afraid I don't understand," I tell him honestly.

"Christ, you're as stupid as they say you are," he bites out, and I think my patience has run thin where he's concerned.

"Your presence is unnecessary at my engagement party," I inform him in my most haughty tone. "Please feel free to leave at any time."

"You don't know who you're messing with, little girl. I could see you ruined," he says, and my mind flashes back to the blackmail letter.

I never heard from them again, and I can't believe I put it out of my head. Could Jeffries be the blackmailer?

"You could try."

"Or you could stop being a dumb bitch for two seconds and tell me how much it will cost for you to get lost and clear the way for my daughter to be the next First Lady of the United States," he snaps.

"That's what this conversation is about?"

"Yes."

I want to laugh. Poor Mr. Jeffries wants me out of Jake's life so his daughter can step into my very expensive shoes. All the while, I'm being blackmailed into being here in the first place. The whole convoluted mess is absolutely ridiculous. One thing is clear though; I can strike Mark Jeffries name off of the "who might be blackmailing me" list.

"I would if I could," I tell him, and as soon as the words are out of my mouth, I wish I could reel them back in.

A month ago, I didn't even want to reach out to Jacob Chancellor for help, even though the pictures that were delivered to my office on that long-ago day involved him too. But now… now, I'm in love with him. And I'm so in love with him that I want to scratch Ashley Jeffries eyes out every time she looks at him. There's no way in hell I'll trade places with her.

Although, she currently has her body—in a very skimpy dress that leaves little to the imagination—plastered to my betrothed's person. I let out a sigh. She's going to be a thorn in my side. I can just feel it.

"If you'll excuse me," I say, turning back to him. "I have other guests to greet."

And then I walk away. I don't walk toward Jake, but that's neither here nor there. I find Jules in a corner of the bar, talking to a man I have never seen before. He's handsome as hell, but their conversation looks anything but friendly.

"Darling!" Jules says, putting a bright smile on her face and turning away from the man in question. "How is the woman of the hour?"

"Good, I think." I laugh.

"Well, if you'll excuse me," the man inserts. "Nice party."

"Thank you."

And then he stalks through the crush of people like a man on a mission.

"Who was that?" I ask.

"No one of importance." After a moment of silence, she caves a little. "So, are you having a wonderful time at your fabulous party?"

"I'm having a time," I answer. "Do you think we could run away and grab a burger?"

"That terrible?"

"This is not my idea of a fun time." I shrug. "Mark Jeffries wants me to clear the path for his daughter to be Jake's FLOTUS."

"Ew. What a lunatic. Sometimes I really hate people," she admits before changing the subject back. "And your idea of a fun time is pajamas and a good book at home with your seven hundred cats."

"I don't have seven hundred cats." I roll my eyes. "I have eight. Eight cats and a giant dog."

"Semantics."

"So, are you having a good time?" I ask her, hoping someone is at least having some fun. I stop myself just short of crossing my fingers before she answers.

"Yes!" she says excitedly. "I met that FBI agent who married the police detective in New Jersey. The one with the mysterious past. And I have them this close to doing an exclusive interview with me."

"That's awesome," I tell her. "I didn't know they were here. I hear she's gorgeous."

"So gorgeous," Jules agrees. "She has black hair and—get this—purple eyes. She's so beautiful it almost hurts to look at her. And so down to earth."

"I love that."

"Me too," Jules murmurs.

"I didn't know Jake knew them…" I trail off, wondering how much more I don't know about him.

"I guess he was on the same SEAL team as Jake and Rick," Jules says. "And her brother. I think there's a story there, but I didn't want to pry. Speaking of Rick, have you seen him and Cara shooting daggers from their eyes at each other from across the room? That is, when they're not eye fucking each other. Seriously, I'm a little hot and bothered just from being in the vicinity."

I laugh, because she's not wrong. "I know what you mean."

"So, Ohio is going to be… fun." And she's not

wrong about that.

"What about Ohio?" Jake asks as he wraps his arms around me from behind. I look over my shoulder at his smiling face. He looks so happy and carefree. It's gestures like this that make me think some of it is real. God, I want it to be real.

"We were just talking about how fun the campaign stops are going to be with the former Mr. and Mrs. at each other's throat," I whisper.

"I think they'll be fine once they fuck it out," Jake replies, and Jules throws her head back and laughs.

"I like you," she says, pointing to him. "And he's not wrong."

"You're both terrible." I roll my eyes.

"Whatever. You love us," she adds.

"Yeah, you love us," Jake repeats bringing my attention back to him. I love at him over my shoulder again and see that twinkle in his eye. He has been trying to get me to admit that I'm in love with him since I may or may not have said anything as I was falling asleep. Or maybe he's just a really good read of people and body language. I don't know. What I do know is he hasn't said he reciprocates the feelings he's been trying so desperately to pull from me. So why should I admit my weakness, when he doesn't suffer from the same affliction?

"You look beautiful, baby," my mom says as they approach our group.

"That she does," Jake agrees.

"My girl is going to make a beautiful bride, Jake," dad warns. "Just see that you deserve her."

"I'll do my best," Jake promises before we say goodbye to my parents, and they head out for the night.

"You ready to get out of here?" Jake asks me before placing a kiss to the side of my head.

"Yeah," I whisper.

The crowd had dwindled in the last hour or so, and the party was officially over. While some still lingered, Jake and I were free to go, and I had been ready to go for hours.

He takes my hand in his and leads me out to the car, where he helps me in and then climbs in after me. I lean back against the seat and close my eyes.

"Tired?" he asks as he brushes a lock of hair back from my face.

"Very."

"It's tough being a blushing bride-to-be," he says, and I can hear the smile in his voice.

"You don't know the half of it," I grumble. "You just get to shower and throw on a suit and show up. What the fuck is that about? I had to spend hours getting ready. And Cara only fed me apples and cheese beforehand! I'm starving."

"Hey, Joe. Can you drive us through the burger joint on the corner?" he asks our driver. And just like that, Jake is anticipating my needs and taking care of me. My heart pangs. I want this to be real. *Please don't let this be an act.* I don't think my heart could handle it if it's all a ruse.

We pick up cheeseburgers and fries for us, Joe, and Gus and then head back to the brownstone. Jake even ordered an extra patty for Sarge. And we eat in the kitchen at the table in our fancy clothes. I wipe my hands off on a napkin before reaching down to pull my heels off my feet one by one.

Jake grabs my ankle in his hands and puts my foot in his lap. He kneads the aches and pains out of my foot before switching to the other one. He sets my foot back on the floor before pushing his chair back to stand, collects all our trash, and tosses it in the receptacle hidden under the sink before walking back to where I'm sitting. When he holds out a hand for me, I take it without questioning it, and then he helps me stand, scoops me up into his arms, and carries me upstairs, leaving my fancy shoes under the kitchen table.

Jake kicks the bedroom door closed behind us before setting me on my feet next to the bed. He turns me around so my back is to him, and one by one, he gently plucks the pins from my hair and tosses them to the nightstand, letting my long hair hang free. He sifts his fingers through it and massages my scalp and neck before dropping his hands to the top of my dress. With nimble fingers, he slides the hidden zipper down my back, letting the material part and fall to the floor before turning me back around to face him.

He reaches around me and unhooks my bra. I let it

slip down my arms and land at my feet before sitting on the edge of the bed. Jake unbuttons his shirt and tosses it away. His belt clanks as he unbuckles it and pushes his pants and underwear to the floor, stepping out of them. The combination of the fire in his eyes and the jerky movements as he sheds his clothes tells me that he is too close to the edge of his control tonight. Whatever emotions he's feeling are riding him hard.

"Lie back," he says, his voice rough.

I scoot to the center of the bed and lean back in the pillows. Jake grabs the waistband of my panties and uses my backward momentum to pull them down my legs before tossing them over his shoulder. I would laugh, but the intensity of his gaze has me shivering instead.

He grips my thighs in his strong hands, spreading them to make room for his broad shoulders to settle in between. I hold my breath in anticipation. And then his breath whispers across my center. I have to close my eyes, the sensations washing over me, owning me, as he licks up my seam.

Jake places open-mouth kisses over my inner thighs and across my mound, letting his stubble scrape against my sensitive skin, before dipping lower to suck my clit into his mouth. I arch my back and rock against his face. He slides a finger inside me and strokes the top.

I twist the bedding in my fingers as Jake rolls his tongue over my clit again and again while he curves his finger inside me. But just when I'm about to come, he pulls back, taking his hand and his mouth away.

"Jake," I plead, but I don't have to beg for long, because he is covering my body with his. I feel his hard tip at my opening, and he slides in deep.

I wrap my legs around his waist and use my heels to try to force him even deeper. He grinds his pelvis between my legs, sending sparks across my skin. I dig my heels in and he does it again, making me moan.

Jake slides his arms underneath me, holding me tight. He tangles one hand in my hair, holding me steady for his mouth to open over mine, and I moan when he licks into my mouth.

I hold on tight to his shoulders as he trails his mouth across my cheek and down my neck, and he sucks the skin at my collarbone, making me arch into him. He soothes the hurt with his tongue before pressing his mouth to mine.

We hold tight to each other while he plunges in and out of my body over and over. So lost in each other, the world begins and ends where our bodies join together. Sweat slicks our skin, and we breathe each other in with his lips so close to mine.

"Please, let this be real," I gasp as he drives into me one more time.

"It's real," he growls just before I shatter, and Jake follows me over the edge, calling out my name as he does.

LOOKS LIKE
AMERICA'S
SWEETHEARTS
ARE HEADED TO
THE WHITE
HOUSE.

NINETEEN

Battle ground

Ohio

One week later...

"I love you," I whisper as Jake plunges slow and deep. This morning he decided to take his sweet time and the slow building, all consuming burn has robbed me of all thoughts.

My eyes go wide as I realize the words I've just said, words I swore I would never say out loud. He presses his mouth to mine and thrusts his tongue between my lips. I cry out as he fucks me in earnest now, harder and faster than the leisure way he made love to me a moment ago.

The way he completely owns me, how he plays my body like no one ever has, chases all thoughts of things that should have been better left unsaid away as we pursue our early-morning orgasms. Jake's measured movements are more frantic now, and I splinter apart in his arms. He drives down one more time before he plants himself deep and spills inside me.

My heart roars in my ears. Our breathing is loud, and his weight presses me down into the bed. But all too soon, reality sets in. I feel my spine stiffen, and I know that he does too. I push on his shoulders so he will let me up and miss his heat the minute the cold air conditioning of the hotel suite hits my overheated skin.

"Grace, we should talk," he says softly as he sits back on his heels. I can't let myself look him in the eyes. I can't see what I know will be waiting for me there—sorrow, because I caught feelings even though this isn't real, and pity, because he doesn't feel the same way. All I know is I will avoid this conversation like I avoid the clap.

"We don't have time," I say, faking a look at the digital clock on the foreign bedside table. Cara will be here soon, and I have to shower."

"Grace—" he starts, but I scramble off the bed.

"Not time!" I shout over my shoulder, and I practically run into the bathroom, where I quickly shut and lock the door. "Shit."

I drop to my knees in front of the toilet and empty my stomach's contents. Stress never was a friend of mine, especially added to the culmination of my life's implosion while on the campaign trail with the man I'm in love with, who doesn't feel the same way. Not to mention, we're in Ohio, the battle ground state, to fight for his chance at the highest office in the nation. It's a lot of pressure, and I'm falling apart.

"Grace, honey," Jake calls out as he knocks on the door. "Are you all right?"

"Yeah, fine," I say just before I flush the toilet and rinse my mouth out in the sink.

"Sweetheart, let me in."

"There's no time, Jake," I say firmly. "I need to shower."

Besides, I really can't let him see me cry right now. I flip the taps on the shower and let the water heat up while I brush my teeth. I wish I had more time to stay in the shower and hide, wallow, whatever it is I need. But I wasn't lying when I said there's no time.

I let it all out, crying in the shower, and then I wash quickly and dry my hair. I pull on a hotel robe and walk out into the living room of the suite where I know Cara wants to set up hair and makeup. I am so worried about avoiding Jake and not making things more awkward while my heart is breaking that I'm surprised by the argument taking place in the suite.

"You are such a son of a bitch," Cara shouts. "Just leave me the hell alone."

"Trust me," Rick bites out. "I would if I could."

"I hate you."

"Not as much as I hate you," he snaps. "How I could have ever loved a cold-hearted bitch like you, I will never know."

"Rick, that's enough," Jake intercede.

"You're right," he says, running an angry hand through his dark hair. "I'll meet you in the car."

Poor Cara. By the look of the beard burn on the side of her neck, they tried to fuck it out last night, just like Jake said they needed, but it appears it didn't help. I guess I'm not the only one here with a bruised heart.

The rest of the morning is spent in silence. After Rick leaves, Jake excuses himself to dress and shower. Cara curls my hair and applies a delicate amount of makeup before I pull on a pink pleated silk skirt that falls just above my knees and a black V-neck cashmere pullover sweater. Cara adds a skinny black patent leather belt around my waist and patent leather Louboutins. Somehow, I keep from bawling like a baby when she hands me Jake's diamond studs to slip in my ears.

Jake appears in a gray suit with an overcoat slung over his arm. He's so effortlessly sexy I can't stand it. He makes my heart skip a beat. I pull on the belted wrap coat that Cara hands me, and when Jake offers me his outstretched hand, I take it in the knowledge I could never hate him. I am in love with him, and I will ride this ride until it ends.

We take the elevator down with Gus. Rick is waiting for us by one of the dark SUVs. He rides with us while Cara and Carter and the rest of our team take the second one. Our cars pull into the underground tunnel of the convention center where the rally is being held.

The news has been showing people waiting to see Jake since late last night. The energy in the area is palpable and thrilling.

Our staff file out of the cars and head into the building to begin prepping and setting up, but Jake waits. He holds me back. I don't want to have this conversation; I'm not ready, but I guess it's now or never.

"I guess I'll see you inside," Rick says before he walks through the doors.

"Don't run," Jake tells me once his friend is gone.

"Jake—" I start, but he doesn't let me finish.

"Just trust me. Give me your trust, and I promise you'll never regret it," he says passionately. "Just don't run."

"Okay."

Once the words are out of my mouth, he grabs me by the back of my neck and hauls me against his body, where he crushes his mouth to mine. The kiss is over before it starts and then Jake is helping me down from the vehicle. The only sign of anything amiss is my slightly smeared lipstick, but Cara can fix that really quick.

The door from the tunnel opens to a concrete hallway that leads to the back rooms of the convention center. The hallways are completely empty, and Jake takes advantage as he pins me to the wall and kisses me again. Gus clears his throat, making us both giggle like teenagers caught making out in a car.

My heart feels so light, so happy. I *am* happy. For the first time since this whole thing began, I think everything is going to work out with Jake. Maybe we got together under unconventional circumstances, but maybe, just maybe, we're meant to be.

As we make our way farther up the hallway, angry words are being shared in hushed tones, but it's clear Cara and Rick are arguing again.

It's also clear I was very wrong. Heartbreakingly wrong. I had foolishly placed my trust in the one person that I knew I shouldn't and I am paying dearly for it now.

"Stop calling me a bitch," she hisses. "I did what I had to do, and I did it for you, you ungrateful bastard."

Rick laughs harshly. "Don't lie. You acted coldly and calculatingly. You thought of nothing but yourself, never thinking of who might get hurt with your actions."

"No, baby," she says snidely. "That's all you. I never stooped so low as to blackmail a woman into being in a relationship with my bestie. You and Chancellor really take the cake."

"I told you that in confidence!" he shouts. "I wanted you to see that I'm not a monster."

"And look around, no one's here to hear it," she says, but when they both turn and look, Jake and I are standing there. My face, which I couldn't control even if I tried, has to show the hurt I'm feeling slashed across it in bold lines.

I look over at Jake, and his face is carefully blank.

It's true. Everything Cara just said is true. I haven't seen the cool politician side of him in the last two months. I guess he was just keeping his true nature locked away.

"Grace," Cara gasps. "I'm so sorry."

"Save it," I snap. I feel numb, but I know it won't last long. I need answers, and then I need to get out of here. "Were you ever going to tell me the truth?"

She swallows audibly but then at least answers me honestly. "No." Thank God, because I couldn't bear it if she lied to me right now.

"And you?" I prompt, turning to Jake. "Were you ever going to tell me the truth?"

"No," he says low. "But Grace—" He starts reaching out for me, but I throw my hands up and back away.

"I told you I loved you!" I scream.

"And I love you!" Jake shouts back.

"No," I say sadly. "You don't. You never once said it until now. Now, when I can't believe a Goddamned thing that comes out of your mouth."

"That's not true and you know it."

"I don't know anything," I trade barbs.

"I have always loved you, but you wouldn't give me the fucking time of day!" he thunders. "What was I supposed to do?"

"Not fuck everything that walked by, Jake!"

"What would you have me do? Become a monk like Rick?" Jake roars. "He hasn't fucked a woman since his wife left him when we were deployed, I'm guessing, until he fucked her last night."

"And look what good that did!" I shout back. "You're both monsters."

"You don't believe that," he says with hurt flashing in his eyes. Even after everything, I hate that I've caused him pain. But he should have been honest with me from the beginning.

"I don't know what to believe anymore," I say sadly. "I have to go."

"No!" Jake growls, but I'm running. I should have ran months ago. Then I wouldn't have lost my heart to a man who cheated to win it. "Grace!"

"No, Jake," I hear Rick say. "Let her go. For now."

I don't stick around to find out what that means. I just run. Like my gut told me to do in the beginning.

I was wrong when I said my heart was breaking this morning, because now it's completely and irrevocably shattered. Maybe it's partly my fault anyway. I had so loved the way he lied.

IS THERE TROUBLE IN PARADISE?

TWENTY

Runaway

Tall Pines, Texas

Three days later

Lights. Lights are bright, and my eyeballs feel like there are shards of glass in them. I suppose crying your eyes out for three days will do that. Not just crying, but the kind of sobbing that is accompanied by screaming and wailing, so my throat feels like I drank too much whiskey while screaming Janis Joplin songs.

That actually doesn't sound like too bad of a plan. I know there's a bar in this town, because I've heard Angie mention it before.

I'm awake. I'm awake, but I don't open my eyes. Maybe if I keep them closed tight enough, this nightmare will go away. But it won't. This nightmare is my life. I finally found a man who checked all of my boxes. He knew me, he really got me in ways that no one ever had before, and he loved me good and well.

"Yeah, Jules," I hear Angie say. "She's here."

I don't want to face Angie yet. I'm not ready. Although, I know she's been ready for the whole sordid tale for days now. All while her sweet husband, Cody, shoots me nervous glances. It's not like a Chinook helicopter is going to materialize out of nowhere in the sky late one night full of special operators in black cargo pants to carry us all away to an unknown location and kill us for knowing their secrets. Jake doesn't have those kinds of connections—*yet*. Although, in less than two weeks, he could very well be President Elect. I haven't bothered to watch the news or pick up a paper, so I have no idea where he is in the polls now.

And then three days ago, I found out it was all a lie. A lie he had orchestrated and had his political henchman help carry out.

"GRACE!" JAKE SHOUTED MY name. He pleaded with me to come back.

"No, Jake," I heard Rick say while he held Jake back. "Let her go. For now."

"Ms. Sanders!" Gus shouted as he ran after me. "Grace! Dammit, stop!"

"No!" I shouted as I ran down the hall. Gus, a former Marine, caught up with me easily before I hit the doors to escape.

"Grace," he said calmly as he shook me gently by the shoulders to get my attention. "You're not thinking clearly."

"I don't want to," I cried. "I just need to go. Let me go. Why can't you just let me go? I have to get out of here."

"I will," Gus said as he held me in his arms like one would a child. "But I need to know you're going to be safe. So clear your head right fucking now."

Gus had never taken that tone of voice with me before, but he's right. I have to clear my head and formulate a plan. And fast. Rick won't hold Jake back for long. And I want to be gone before he lets go.

I let out a shaky breath to try to quell my rising panic. "You're right. What do I do?"

"We're going to get you to the car rental outside this town and then you're going to drive to a private airport and board a flight back to New York, where I will have an agent waiting to meet you," Gus explains. I nodded. I needed to get to a car rental place, but I wasn't going back to New York, at least not then.

"Okay," I lied to one of the few people I still respected. "I'll follow your lead."

"Let me radio the other agents on the premises and update them," he said before touching his clear earpiece I never noticed with the tip of his index finger. "This is Raider. I have the Nightingale and am moving her to an alternate location. Ghost needs coverage. Monk has his hands full."

There was so much there that I couldn't even begin to decipher it, so I didn't. I don't care anymore. Jacob Chancellor had my heart, and he smashed it to pieces.

"Let's go," Gus said to me before loading me into one of the SUVs.

"Thank you."

Gus got behind the wheel and drove me for forty-five minutes to just outside the town we were in, where no one would recognize me. At least, I hoped not. Gus walked me into the small car rental agency and helped me procure a car, mainly by handing me my purse so I could hand over my ID and credit card.

Once a small SUV with all the bells and whistles including GPS was brought around, I climbed in the driver's seat. Gus stood over me like a big brother. I needed to remind myself that he works for Jake and not me. Everyone was loyal to Jake, and by way of that awful token, not a one was loyal to me. Even Cara. When the hurt has eased a bit and the fog clears, I was sure I'll realize she was stuck in an unfortunate situation. But that's a song for another time.

"Remember," he said. "Go straight to the airport. I've plugged it into the GPS for you already."

"Thank you," I replied and meant it. He got me out of there when I needed it.

He shut the door, and I buckled my seatbelt before starting the engine. I waved to Gus, who stood on the curb, ready to head back to his duties to the senator, and I merged onto the highway. I drove two exits up the highway in the direction of the airport when I spotted a big warehouse store. I pulled into the parking lot, checking my mirrors the whole time. My phone rang, but I didn't reach for it. I didn't care anymore.

I grabbed my bag from the passenger seat and ran inside. I pulled a shopping cart from the rack, dropped my bag in the baby seat, and headed for the women's section. I pulled leggings, tees, a ball cap, and sweatshirts from the bargain racks. A pack of cotton panties and a couple plain cotton bras like the one I had worn under my sheer engagement dress were next, my heart panging at the thought of the beautiful photo that still sits on the front page of every news site.

My phone buzzed in my bag.

I grabbed a bag of plain white socks and then pushed my cart to the shoe department. I picked a pair of cheap white sneakers and moved on to the beauty section. I loaded up a toothbrush, face wash, a comb, deodorant, and a box of tampons before heading to the register. I checked out quickly and hurried into the ladies' room, where I don the leggings, tee, sweatshirt, and ball cap.

My phone buzzed again, and I pulled it out of my bag. I had five missed phone calls from Jules, eight from Cara, three from Rick, and forty-seven from Jake. When he didn't get through calling, he began texting.

JAKE: Call me.

JAKE: It's not what you think.

JAKE: Baby, I love you. Please call me.

My heart clenched at his saying he loved me. If he loved me, he wouldn't have fucking lied to me. How could he do this to me? To us?

JAKE: Dammit, please call me.

JAKE: Don't do this, Grace.

The kicker was the next message. Guilt poured through me. But how could he accuse me of giving up on us when he never even gave us a chance to begin with?

JAKE: You promised you wouldn't run.

JAKE: Gus says you're not at the airport. Damn it, Grace. Don't do anything stupid.

JAKE: Please, just come back to me. I'll explain everything.

JAKE: Pick up the phone, Grace.

JAKE: Rick says they have a ping on your phone. Gus is coming for you. I promise I'll never lie or withhold the truth from you again. Just come back to me.

JAKE: Don't run.

Shit! I couldn't wait around to find out how this drama would end, so I did what Jake just told me not to do—I ran. But not before I dropped my brand-new cell phone on the floor of a Walmart bathroom and stomped it beneath my sneaker-clad heel.

Then I walked away, leaving it behind.

I tucked my purchases in the trunk of the rental car and climbed in the driver seat, heading in the complete wrong direction from Jake, from the airport, from just about everything I knew. Instead, I headed south.

Eventually, I stopped to fill up the gas tank and grab some coffee. The idea of food turned my stomach, so I didn't even try. I reprogrammed the GPS for a small town in East Texas and headed for friends who loved me so much they might as well have been family.

I stole away like a runaway.

"I KNOW YOU'RE AWAKE," Angie says from the doorway. "You wanna talk about it?"

"No." My voice is rough. It sounds harsh and unused.

"Well, good," Angie's aunt, Mable, says from the doorway, pushing past her. "That means there's a juicy story behind it."

"You wanna talk about the sexy senator who's been calling the house every day?" Angie pushes.

"Also no." God, please just make it all go away. When my heart stops hurting so badly, I'll go back to my life and I'll never let another man make me weak again.

"He's real hot. Almost as good-looking as the congressman from here. You know the one?" Mable asks like we talk about how hot the man who broke my heart is every day. "The hottie with the one eye. I think he was a Navy SEAL too. Those Navy SEALs are crazy hot. I'd bag one."

"Dammit, Mable!" Angie yells.

"What?" she asks like she's not even bothered by her niece yelling at her. "Like you wouldn't hit that."

"I'm still here, ladies," Cody says.

"Well, what in the hell for?" Mable gripes. "We have girl shit to talk about, and by the looks of her, it's some heavy shit. Heeea-vy. Shit. I'd break out the tequila, but she's had a box of tampons sitting un-opened on the bathroom counter since she got here, so I'm thinking Aunt Flo went south for winter and she's about as good and knocked up as you are."

I feel my eyes pop open. No. It can't be. I can't be. I can't be having the baby of the man who betrayed me. Life can't be that unfair, can it?

"No," I whisper. I count through the weeks in my head.

"See?" Mable tells Cody. "Heavy. Shit."

"Maybe we should call the senator back," he says. "I'm too pretty for prison."

"That you are," both women agree, rolling their eyes.

I burst into tears when I realize how far back I've counted.

"See?" Mable chirps. "Pregnant."

"Maybe I'm just late, because I've been under so much stress," I hedge. Periods are weird. They do that sometimes. I'm pretty sure I read an article in Cosmo about that. Everything will be fine.

"Uhh… sure," Angie says. "That's totally how it works."

"So, is it really that bad?" Cody asks.

"He lied to me," I answer.

"Well no one can tell the truth all the time," Mable explains. "That would be boring."

Cody and Angie both shoot Mable a withering glare.

"He blackmailed me into being in a relationship with him," I tell them. "I didn't know it was him at the time though. I thought he was helping me out of a bad spot. And then I fell in love with him."

"Was he mean to you?" Angie asks me.

"No."

"Did he hit you? Beat you? Talk ugly to you?" Mable asks.

"No, none of that."

"Well, then what's the problem?"

"Really?" I ask sharper than I meant to. "Were none of you listening?"

"Honey," Cody starts, and I flinch at the term of endearment Jake seems to favor. If he notices, he doesn't let on that he does; he just presses forward. "Men do really stupid shit all the time."

"This is true," Angie agrees.

"Even the very best of us," he says. "No one is perfect."

"Except me," Mable inserts, making Angie roll her eyes. "And God."

"I'm really tired," I tell them, hoping some of the sweetest people I've ever met can take a hint.

"I'm going to fix you a sandwich," Angie says before she waddles her very pregnant body out of the room.

"I'll go into town and pick up a bottle of tequila and a pregnancy test," Mable says helpfully. "Oh, and some vitamins. Then you'll know which you need more after you pee on the stick."

And then she's gone too. Only Cody remains.

"You going to be all right, kid?" he asks in his slow Texas drawl.

"Eventually."

"You want me to kick his ass?" he adds, making me smile my first real smile in who knows how many days. It feels brittle and unused but I still enjoy it all the same. "I was a badass pro football player, you know."

"He was a Navy SEAL."

"Well fuck that, then," he answers. "This face is too pretty to pulverize."

"It's the thought that counts," I tell him, and then he's gone too and I'm left alone with my thoughts.

Could I ever forgive Jake? Do I even want to try? And what if I am pregnant? That would change everything. I'm not going to think about that one for now. Now, I just need to know if I can trust Jake again, and if so, can I let myself continue to love him? Because my heart is telling me that I never stopped.

On that thought, I yawn. Maybe it wasn't a lie after all.

WHERE IS GRACE?

TWENTY-ONE

Abandon ship—all is lost

Jake

My head is pounding.

My head is pounding, and I stink. My stomach flips and flops. I'm probably going to puke soon, but it's no less than I deserve.

A heavy knock sounds on the front door, but I don't bother to answer it. I don't want to see anyone at all. Not since Grace walked out of my life and didn't come back. She didn't forgive me, wouldn't listen to the truth.

I hear the front door open and someone key in the code for the alarm. This is unfortunate for a multitude of reasons, but the one at the top of my list is that I don't want to see anyone, and I definitely don't want anyone to see me like this.

Or maybe this is my new normal, and everyone else can get bent. Who knows?

"What the fuck?" Lee calls out.

"Fuck off."

"Brother, did you sleep on the couch?" Wes asks me.

"Yes."

"Why?" he follows up. He knows. I know he knows, because he's married now, but at one point in time, he was where I am now. Not to say that he black-mailed his wife into a relationship anonymously, but he did break up with her when she was only eighteen when he realized he couldn't move her to San Diego only to be deployed all the fucking time—which we definitely were back in the day.

"You don't want to know." I eye him suspiciously.

"Oh, I think we do," Rick chimes in, the fucking fuck. Seriously, I think I hate him.

"I can't sleep in the bed without Grace," I admit.

"There it is!" Wes cheers. "What do we have for our winner?"

"Heartache." Lee laughs.

"Like you're one to talk," I mutter rudely. I'm mad and I'm hurt, and if I'm being totally honest, I'm a little drunk still, so I'm lashing out at anyone who reminds me of what a total fuckup I am.

"This is true," Wes says with a smile. He's clearly enjoying Lee dangling on a line like he is.

"Is the sexy medical examiner still not talking to you?" Rick asks.

"Oh, she's not only not talking to him," Wes adds. "She's knocked up."

"Is it yours?" I ask.

"No," Lee growls. "But who the fuck cares? If she gave me even the tiniest bit of hope, I'd be there for her and raise that baby like it was my own fucking blood."

"I'm sorry, brother," I reply quietly. He doesn't deserve my shit. "Punch Wes again. That'll make us both feel better."

"Hey!" Wes shouts. "That is uncalled for."

"He's the one fucking your sister," I add with a boy-scout smile. "I never fucked your sister. Scout's honor."

"Neither did I," Rick says with an evil smirk.

"Stop talking about fucking my sister, you assholes, or I'll punch every one of you," Lee growls.

"Why me?" Wes asks.

"Because you are fucking her!"

"I married her!" he shouts back and fuck if I hadn't missed this when we all went our separate ways.

"Let's get back on track here, gentlemen," Rick says. "Someone just needs to kick Ghost's ass so he can go claim his girl and win an election."

"Hooyah!" they all shout at the same fucking time.

"Abandon all hope, sailors. All is lost," I tell them

sadly and fuck me if I don't sound pitiful even to my own ears.

"Wow," Lee says. "I thought you were a SEAL."

"And not a pussy," Wes adds.

"Do SEALs quit?" Rick asks.

"No, sir!" they all shout.

"When are the easy days?" Wes prompts, and they all pause and wait for me to answer them, and fuck it if I don't have a little hope that maybe I can right this ship and fix my life.

"Yesterday," I answer them. "The only easy day was yesterday."

"Hooooyah!"

"Now hit the fucking shower, Captain," Lee says, falling into his old routine. "You smell like whiskey and desperation."

"Fuck you." I laugh as I head for the shower, flipping them off on my way. "Someone book me a flight to Tall Pines."

"Where the fuck is that?" Wes asks.

"The middle of fucking nowhere," Rick answers.

"It's everything," I correct him. "It's the most important place right now."

"That it is, brother," Rick says solemnly. "Take it from me; when you find your missing piece, the other part of your fucking soul, grab it with both hands and never let it go."

"Roger that."

He doesn't have to tell me twice.

Batten down the hatches, Grace, because I'm coming for you, and I won't give up. Not fucking ever.

She's my everything. I should have told her five years ago that I thought she was amazing. I should have chased after her then with ruthlessness, but parts of me were still too dark. I had seen too much; there was too much blood on my hands. She was too clean and pure, and I didn't deserve her. I still don't deserve her, but I won't walk away. It's like Rick said—she's the other half of my soul, the very best parts of me, the one who makes me want to be a better fucking man.

With her, I am everything. Without her, I am nothing.

Sure, I could keep breathing, keep my heart beating without her, but I would just be existing like I have been for the last three days. I want to live. I want to live for her. I want to love her like she deserves and, hand to God, if she gives me another chance, I will make sure she never regrets it for the rest of her life.

I love her that much.

IT'S A LANDSLIDE.

TWENTY-TWO

Got my vote

I am a horrible human being.

That's really my only excuse right now. A couple days with Mable and Angie have made me realize that while Jake was wrong to deceive me like he did, I was also wrong in not hearing him out. I was not the bigger person.

If I really love him like I have claimed to, then I should have given him the chance to explain. I'm going to have to go to him when I get back to New York and talk to him. He may not forgive me, and I may not forgive him either. I can't tell until I hear what he has to say, and only then will I make my judgement, like I should have done all along.

And I do love him. If I didn't, I wouldn't feel like

absolute shit. My heart just hurts.

Cody's German Shepherd and I meander through the property. I've been taking walks here and there with the older dog. It makes me miss Sarge and the cats. I hope Jake has taken care of them. Although, I know that he has. Deep down, I know he is a good guy. Jake would never let anything happen to my babies.

In truth, I hope Sarge is looking after him. I was awful. When Steve and I get back to the house, I'm going to call Rick and check the polls. I can't be the reason Jake loses, and he would make such an amazing president. I just hope it's not too late. Election day is just a week away. The American people believed in Jake before I came along, and I've got a week to show them they were absolutely right.

"Let's head back, Steve. I've got some work to do," I tell the dog. He just looks at me and groans. "And a new phone to buy. I can't believe I destroyed a two-thousand-dollar phone."

Steve just growls.

"Anybody ever tell you that you're very judgy?"

"All the damn time," Cody says, making me laugh when we walk up the porch. "There's someone here to see you. I could beat him up, but his Secret Service agent could kick my ass and is madder than a wet hen at you. So, you decide if I need another back surgery or not."

"I'm not going to get you beaten up." I roll my eyes at his drama. Over the last few days, I've learned that the giant retired football player is kind of a big girl in a very loveable way.

"So you're going into the lion's den then?" he asks me.

"Yeah, I think I am."

"Atta girl," he says.

"You don't rock a football coach vibe at all," I tell him with my eyes wide and an innocent look on my face before I burst out laughing.

"You're ridiculous," he grumbles with a smile on his face.

"Jules is worse," I tell him as I make my way into the house. "Wait until you meet her!"

But the smile slides off my face when I see Jake sitting on the couch. He jumps up to stand when I walk in the room, ever the gentleman. His clothes are clean and his jaw is shaved, but he looks tired. He's wearing worn jeans and a T-shirt, with a pair of running shoes on his feet. He's dressed casually, but he looks as handsome as ever. Actually, Jake looks like I feel. And then I remember I'm not dressed in my usual Chanel and Louboutins either. I'm in leggings and sneakers and a Texas A&M sweatshirt I borrowed from Cody. My hair is in a ponytail, and the Cleveland baseball cap I bought in Ohio is on my head. My face is free of makeup.

"Hi," I say shyly before brushing a lock of hair behind my ear.

"Hi," he greets. "Can we talk?"

"Yes." I make my way over to sit on the opposite end of the sofa from him. Jake sits and bounces his knee. It's the only outward sign of his agitation.

Steve growls at him.

"Is that dog winking at me?" he asks.

"Shh!" I hush him quickly. "He only has one eye, and he doesn't like it when people stare."

"Oh," he stumbles a bit. "I'm sorry."

"It's okay," I tell him, and it clearly is, because Steve lies down on his dog bed with a groan.

"He kind of reminds me of Sarge," Jake says. "He's not happy with me right now."

"Oh no, is he okay? He hasn't fallen back into his depression, has he?" Shit, another life I've ruined by being a drama llama, as Jules would say.

"He's fine," Jakes says with a smile. "He blames me for you not coming home. Your cat shits in my shoes every day now, by the way."

I bark out a laugh. "I'm sorry."

"No, you're not," he says.

"No, I'm not," I agree.

We sit there quietly, neither of us knowing what to say. I pick at the cuticle on my thumb nail, and Jake just watches me.

"I'm sorry," we both say at the same time and laugh. It's awkward and nervous and not at all like we used to be around each other. I hate it immediately.

"I am sorry," I admit and then decide I'm in for a penny, so I might as well be in for a pound. "I wasn't fair to you. "I told you that I… cared about you. And then I did not treat you the way I should have, and I am sorry."

"You don't have anything to apologize for," he says, and his voice is rough with deep emotion. "It was me, all me, and I never should have put you in the position I did."

"Oh… that position wasn't all bad," I reply, and my eyes go wide when I realize how my words sound. "What I mean is—"

"I remember a few positions you really like." He smirks that panty melting smirk that got me into this mess to begin with.

I roll my eyes. "You're ridiculous."

"Yes." Jake glances away before looking back at me, and his blue eyes burn into mine. "I was attracted to you when I first came home, but I wasn't ready. I had been living in darkness for too long, and you were too bright. I couldn't sully that with the blood on my hands."

His words break my heart, and I want him to stop talking, but I also want Jake to feel like he can share his burdens with me. I'll help him carry them.

"And then when I was almost ready and definitely tired of waiting," he says in a self-deprecating tone, "you wouldn't give me the time of day. I kept thinking you'd warm up to me, but you never did."

"I'm sorry. I should have given you the chance then. You're a good man, Jake Chancellor, and I wish I hadn't wasted the time."

"I'm not a good man," he says, and when I open my mouth to stop him, he holds up a hand to ask me to let him finish. "No, let me say this. I'm not a good man. I'm not a bad man either. I've done things I'm not proud of for the sake of my country and the mission, but they are also things that leave dark marks on your soul. I have also done things in the name of politics that I am not wholly proud of. But if you give me another chance, I promise they will never touch you. I will never lie or mislead you again. There will be things that I won't be able to tell you, but I will be honest about that. If you take another chance on me, we will be partners. I will make sure you never regret being mine again for the rest of your life. So what do you say?"

"Yes," I whisper.

"Yes?"

"Yes," I tell him. "But your dark marks will touch me, because you're mine and I love you. I don't want you to have to suffer alone. I don't want you to suffer at all. I love you."

He closes his eyes tight, and when he opens them again, the blue is so bright it sears me where I sit. "I love you too."

"Yeah?" I ask, tucking that hair behind my ear

again.

"Yeah," he confirms. "I've been in love with you for a while."

"But what about all the—" I stop the words from coming out of my mouth, but it's a little too late. I am such an idiot.

"The other women?" Jake finishes for me.

"Forget I said anything."

"I was an idiot," Jake admits. "I couldn't have you and it hurt."

"I'm sorry I hurt you."

"I'm sorry I hurt you too, Grace," he says, scooting closer and closer to me on the sofa, inch by inch. "So damn sorry. I'm going to kiss you now."

"Okay," I whisper, and then he does. Jake presses his lips down to mine and it's tentative and sweet… and then it isn't. I've missed him so much I grip the front of his T-shirt in my fists. I can't get close enough to him. And then he pulls back and drops his forehead to mine.

"I didn't come out here to make out with you on the couch of a retired pro ballplayer. Did you know that's who your friend married?" he asks me. "Dude is a legend."

"Yeah, I knew, but Jules and I aren't big football fans," I say, watching his face. "I take it you are?"

"I am, but not as much as baseball. I love baseball," he tells me. "Can I take you to a game sometime?"

"I'd love that."

"Me too," he says softly. "Look, I know we have a lot to work on and talk out, but I want you to know I'm willing to put in the work."

"Okay," I reply, not really understanding where he's going with this.

"Don't make me leave Texas without you," Jake pleads. "I need you, honey. I think I always have. That's why I gave you a family heirloom for your engagement ring." I look to the ring on my finger. Apparently, Jules was right when she said he gave me a meaningful ring because he loved me. I've never been so glad to have been wrong.

"I need you too. I'll come home with you."

"Thank fuck," he groans before pressing his mouth to mine. "It doesn't have to be right now, but know I am going to marry you. When you're ready."

"Well, it's not going to be soon," I tell him, and his face falls. "We've got an election to win. After that, there will be plenty of time to get married."

"Okay," he says, his face brightening.

"Okay," I agree. "Take me home, Jake."

"Gladly."

Jake takes my hand in his and leads me out of the house.

"I'm going home, Cody," I announce over my shoulder.

"It's about time," he says. "See you around, yankee."

Outside, Gus pulls open the door to the SUV for me. "Thanks, Gus."

"I'm still mad at you," he says.

"I'm sorry, Gus."

"I accept your apology. Do it again and I'll tell the boss," he threatens as Jake climbs in behind me.

"And the boss spanks," Jake adds.

I just roll my eyes. "Shusssh," I say, covering his mouth with my hand, which only makes him laugh harder. "They'll hear you, and then we'll never get anyone to vote for you."

"He's got my vote," Gus says.

"And he's got mine," Joe chimes in.

"Aw, that's sweet, guys."

"And what about you?" Jake asks as he leans into me. "Do I have your vote?"

"Nah, I really like the other guy." I wink.

"The… the… the other guy?" he sputters. "You wound me, woman."

"Nah, I suspect your ego is just fine."

"Speaking of other guys…" Jake starts.

"Yeah?"

"Whose fucking sweatshirt are you wearing? Because it sure as hell isn't mine," he growls, making me laugh. Jake and I are going to be just fine. "I'm as serious as a heart attack right now, Grace."

"I know you are. It's Cody's. We're going to have to mail it back. Angie is quite fond of stealing it. She only let me wear it, because I looked so pitiful."

"Well that's all right, I suppose."

"So, how are we in the polls? What do we need to work on?" I ask, and I only ask more and more questions the whole way home—that is, until Jake showed me the bedroom on the private plane. Then I didn't ask any questions at all.

And when we landed, Rick was all too happy to talk about the final strategy with me. Somewhere along the way, he became my champion, and we formed a tentative truce. I like it. I think I like Rick. What the fuck is happening to my life? This is bananas. But I wouldn't have it any other way.

And the next week, we were all standing by Jake's side when the results were finally in.

He won by a landslide.

CHEERS TO THE NEW
PRESIDENT.

EPILOGUE

Here's to you, Mr. President

January

"Please stand here, Ms. Sanders. Palms up to support the Kennedy Bible," Chief Justice quietly tells me.

It's freezing. One would think being a native New Yorker would have prepared me for how cold Washington is in January, but it didn't. Thankfully, Cara decked me out in a stunning teal dress with a beautiful winter-white belted wrap coat. I have tan leather gloves on my hands and these amazing stockings that look sheer but are actually fleece-lined, so I'm good. The gloves are in my coat pocket out of respect for the Kennedy Bible.

Jake looks handsome as he stands across from me in a dark-gray suit with a white shirt and a blue tie. He has a darker gray wool overcoat on and black leather gloves, which he removed to place his hand on the famous book as well—a nod to the fact that he held the infamous senate seat previously held by none other than John Fitzgerald Kennedy in the state of New York.

When he raises his right hand and takes his oath of office, his voice rings proud and strong.

"I do solemnly swear that I will faithfully execute the Office of President of the United States, and will to the best of my ability, preserve, protect, and defend the Constitution of the United States. So help me God."

"AND NOW, THE PRESIDENT and First Lady of the United States," Rick says as Jake leads me onto the dance floor and pulls me into his arms.

He looks so dashing in a crisp black tux with his Navy medals mounted on his chest. I love that he is proud of who he is and how hard he worked to get here. It's a nod to the sacrifices that were made before he took this next mission.

Rick is similarly dressed. And speaking of Rick, he has a new job title. As of this morning, Jake officially named him Chief of Staff. The pitbull of politics has a new post to guard. He and Cara are still circling each other. I'm hoping they figure things out soon.

I am wearing the same light-pink dress with gold beading that knocked Jake's sock off the first time, and I've gotten a ton of compliments on it, not only because it's fantastic, but because I'm so "fiscally conservative." I barely held in my hilarity over that one. If only they could see my shoe closet.

I look over his shoulder and see Jules sneaking off with a Marine officer. Oh, Jules… I can't see his face, but at least he has a nice ass. Go girl! One day, she will stop toying with men and settle down. I just don't think it'll happen in the next four years. She also has a new job description. Jake was so impressed with her handling of the oil spill in the Gulf Coast that he named her Press Secretary. She promptly put in her resignation with Eagle News Network. They were sad to see her go, but they understood that this was the opportunity of a lifetime.

"A wedding should be easier to plan after an inaugural ball," he says, pulling me in close as we circle the dance floor. "Don't you think?"

"I do."

"That's the right idea." He laughs at his own joke.

"Always a joker," I say, rolling my eyes.

"I was thinking of a June wedding at Camp David. What about you?" he asks me.

"I think you're going to be disappointed," I tell him hesitantly.

"Why's that?" Jake questions. "Are you changing your mind already? Sorry you didn't back the other guy?"

"Never," I say honestly. "But I was thinking more along the lines of February in D.C."

"Any reason why?" he asks. "Don't get me wrong; sooner than later has always been my preference. But why now?"

"Because we're going to be very busy in June," I answer cryptically.

"Oh yeah? With what?"

"A baby," I whisper in his ear. "I'm pregnant."

"A baby," he murmurs, and I can't tell if he's happy or shocked or maybe a little of both.

"Are you happy?" I ask him, suddenly I'm feeling a little nervous even though in my heart, I know that I have nothing to worry about.

"This is by far the best day of my life," he says. "And it's all because of you. I love you."

"Here's to you, Mr. President."

"And to you, Mrs. Chancellor."

And then we shocked the attendees when he crushed his lips to mine and spun me about the room. Rick just laughed. Cara looked sad, but I'm not losing hope for them yet. And Jules and her mystery man were long gone.

As for Jake and me, we've got all we ever wanted.

THE END

Thank you so much for reading ***The Senator's Secret!*** I hope you enjoyed Jake and Grace as much as I enjoyed writing them. Next up is Cara and Rick's story, ***Caught by the Chief of Staff.***

If you would like to get to know Claire and Wes more, you can follow their story in the ***Claire Goodnite Series.*** And for more from Angie, Cody, and Mable, you can read their story, ***Stand***, now.

PLAYLIST

Dirty Little Secret—All American Rejects

Fortunate Son—CCR

Beautiful People—Ed Sheeran ft.

Bad Guy—Billie Eilish

Classic—MKTO

I Don't Care—Ed Sheeran ft. Justin Bieber

End Game—Taylor Swift ft. Ed Sheeran and Future

New York at Night—Old Dominion

Come Over—Sam Hunt

Halo—Beyoncé

Everything I Wanted—Billie Eilish

Love the Way You Lie—Eminem ft. Rhianna

When the Party's Over—Billie Eilish

Someone You Loved—Lewis Capaldi

My 4 Letters—Brielle Von Hugel

ALSO BY JENNIFER

A Presidential Affair
The Senator's Secret
Caught by the Chief of Staff
The Press Secretary's Passion

The Claire Goodnite Series
Tell Me a Story
Tuck Me in Tight
Say a Sweet Prayer
Kiss Me Goodnight
By the Light of the Moon
The Complete Claire Goodnite Series

The Liam Goodnite Series
Hush Little Baby
Don't Say a Word

The Funerals and Obituaries Series
I Met a Girl
Dead and Buried
Dead and Gone
Dead and Deceived
Dead and ... Wed?

The Murder on Ice Series
Attack Zone
Layback

The Southern Heartbeats
Stand, Volume 1
Joy
Whiskey Lullaby, Volume 2
Mercy
Just a Dream, Volume 3, Coming 2021

Stand Alone Titles
Trap: A Salvation Society Novel

ABOUT THE AUTHOR

Jennifer is a thirty-something lover of words, all words: the written, the spoken, the sung (even poorly), the sweet, the funny, and even the four-letter variety. She is a native of San Diego, California where she grew up reading the Brownings and *Rebecca* with her mother and *Clifford and the Dog who Glowed in the Dark* with her dad, much to her mother's dismay.

Jennifer is a graduate of California State University San Marcos, where she studied Criminology and Justice Studies. She is also a member of Alpha Xi Delta.

Thirteen years ago, she was swept off her feet by her very own sailor. Today, they are happily married, and the parents of an eleven-year-old and nine-year-old twins. She lives in East Texas, where she can often be found on the soccer or baseball fields, drawing with her children, reading, or wondering what the hell her favorite senior citizens have gotten up to now. Jennifer is convinced that if she puts her Fitbit on one of the dogs, she might finally make her step goals.

She loves a great romance, an alpha hero, and lots and lots of laughter.

(She loves that shit)

Website
www.jenniferrebeccaauthor.com

Facebook
www.facebook.com/JenniferRebeccaAuthor

Instagram
www.instagram.com/JenniferRebeccaAuthor

Twitter
www.twitter.com/JenniRLreads

Pinterest
www.pinterest.com/JenniferRebeccaAuthor

Bookbub
www.bookbub.com/authors/jennifer-rebecca

Book+Main
www. bookandmainbites.com/JenniferRebecca

And join her reader group on Facebook:
The Dangerous Dames
www. facebook.com/groups/JRdangerousdames

PRESIDENTIAL
BOOK TWO

CAUGHT
BY THE
CHIEF of STAFF

I clutch my phone in my hand so tightly I'm afraid the glass will shatter, and then where will I be? I just stopped the video. I'm going to be sick, but I can't now. I have to get to Rick. If anyone can fix this, it's him. I know we have a lot to atone for between us, but I know I can trust him with this.

My lungs burn with the air that isn't filling them as I race from the residence to the offices. I was just coming by to check on Grace. She has an appearance tomorrow, and we needed to get everything squared away. I love being her stylist, and life in D.C. totally agrees with my daughter Rachel and me.

Or so I thought. Now, I'm regretting every decision that led me here.

"Stop, ma'am," one of the Marines who guards the offices says. "No one is allowed back here."

"I need to see Rick Donovan right away," I tell him as I flash my badge. My voice is trembly and my hands shake. "It's an emergency."

"Right this way, Ms. Donovan," Gus, one of Jake's Secret Service agents, says. "You can wait in his office. I'll tell him you're here."

"Can't I just go to him?" I ask. "It's important."

"No, ma'am. He's in a closed-door meeting," Gus explains.

"Oh okay," I say. "Just… please hurry."

I pace Rick's office over and over while I wait for him. If he doesn't show soon, I'm going to puke in his wastepaper basket. The offending video on my phone plays in my brain on a loop. These things are time-sensitive, right? And my baby. I can't bear for her to be away from me for one more minute.

"What the fuck could be so important you've interrupted me during a closed-door meeting, Cara? Did you break a nail?" he seethes. I know he hates me; I hate me too. I did things he will never understand to protect him, to protect Rachel, and now it was all for nothing.

"She's gone," I whisper. The words get stuck in my throat and I can barely get them out.

"Who's gone?" he asks, his body instantly alert.

"Our daughter," I explain, holding out my phone with the video cued up. "Somebody took Rachel."

"I think I know who did it," Rick says after a moment.

"You do?" I breathe. "Well, go get her. We have to

get her back."

"I'll get Rachel back if it's the last thing I do," he vows.

God, I hope it's not. He and Rachel need time to get to know each other after spending almost nine years apart. I don't want anything to happen to either of them. I love them both, and I always have.

"Please," I beg. I hope he knows I mean I need him to get our daughter back, but I also need him to come back in one piece as well.

"I don't know exactly who it is, but I think I know why."

"What? Why?" I question.

"Someone is trying to blackmail the president, and the only way to get to him is through me."

And then I promptly throw up in the wastebasket after all.

ACKNOWLEDGEMENTS

Thank you so much for reading THE SENATOR'S SECRET!!! I hope you loved it as much as I enjoyed writing it. There is so much more in store for the gang including your very favorite president.

I can't thank my partner in crime, Alyssa Garcia, enough. She wears many hats: designer, boss lady, marketing guru, publicist, and I would be lost without her. She openly admits that she has wanted this book more than any other I have written and I'm okay with that. She balances me in ways I couldn't imagine. Our planning meetings are my favorite.

You can read the words that I write because Kayla Robichaux can make sense of my ramblings. She didn't bat an eye when I said I'm in the market for an editor but I'm dyslexic/ dysgraphic and it's going to be a tough job. Along the way she also became a dear friend and I am forever grateful.

The magician behind the curtain of everything is my amazing assistant, Tricia Crouch. I have absolutely no worries because I know she's got my back and has joined Alyssa in her love of a spreadsheet. While writing this book, she jumped into the role of magazine manager with complete perfection. Alyssa and I would die without her.

And thank you to my very own girl gang, Alyssa, Stacy, and Emma, who when I had a crazy idea to jump head first into dark romantic suspense they helped me